TURNING OF THE BONES

& OTHER STORIES

MIKE X WELCH

DUSKBOUND
BOOKS

TURNING OF THE BONES
& OTHER STORIES

Mike X Welch

Illustrations by Tom Rolland

Some of the stories contained herein have been previously published in other anthologies; many have been edited or expanded from the versions in those collections.

This is a work of fiction. Names, characters, businesses, places, events, locales, and incidents are either the products of the author's imagination or used in a fictitious manner. Any resemblance to actual persons, living or dead, or actual events is purely coincidental. Except for the part about the wolves. The wolves are real. They know who they are and what they've done. Go ahead, send a lupine lawyer after me. Bring it. This isn't even close to over yet.

ISBN: 979-8-9897478-3-2

First Edition © 2024 **Mike X Welch**

DEDICATION

E.R. Baxter III – Rest in peace, sir, and thank you for teaching me.

Dan Sinclair – Here or there, always in my thoughts, Batch.

Tom Rolland – Lang may yer lum reek.

FOREWORD

Thank you for holding my book in your hands. I want to get that out of the way right off the bat. Nothing I say here means a thing unless you're reading it. I will never forget it; the covenant between author and reader is sacred to me.

Not much else is, however.

My hope is that you'll come to know me as an author who can be transgressive without having to resort to shock. Someone who will grab you by the feelings and shake you until our safe word tumbles from your quivering tongue. Someone who will make you laugh, make you cry, make you want to come back for more.

Hi. My name is Mike X Welch, and I'm a writer.

We managed to establish the above with my first collection, *ENAN-TIODROMIA: collected stories*, released by my own bad self in early 2020. Early 2020 will go down in history as quite possibly the worst time to self-release and promote...well, anything, really. But, thanks to readers like you, that tiny book reached a broad audience and currently holds a solid 4.5 star rating on Amazon. Awesome people from the US to Canada to Australia, the UK, and Malta (!) have reviewed the book favorably. Ah, would that I could embrace each and every one of you, all those pesky restraining orders be damned.

Some of you will notice that there are three stories here that also appeared in *ENANTIODROMIA*. Here's where I need to clarify some stuff: "You Might Get It" and "Tuesdays with Moran'd'arth" appear largely unchanged from versions you may have already read. However, "Turning of the Bones" is presented here in a greatly expanded version. Due to its popularity, I decided to flesh out the story and add some lore and detail, primarily at the front half of the tale. I would like to think I've changed it for the better, but only you can truly decide. Along the way, the story placed in the Top Ten of the 2021 Launch Pad Prose Contest and, more importantly, led to me crossing paths with a handsome Scotsman named Tom Rolland.

Tom's illustrations are featured liberally in this book, and I couldn't be more proud to have them. Tom and I have one of those connections that defies logic; despite the fact that only one of us speaks passable English, we were finishing each other's sentences within a week or so of meeting. My hat is off to Tom for putting up with my shortcomings. Anyhoo, Tom and I have decided to turn "Turning of the Bones" into a graphic novel, also known as a "long-form comic book" to people who don't buy or read graphic novels. It will be adult. It will be dark. It will be unflinching. And it will also be a minor miracle if it comes out during either Tom's or my lifetime.

Assuming that "Turning of the Bones" ~~the musical~~ the graphic novel is actually published and does well, we're thinking about releasing another graphic novel of my short stories. That's right – if you've ever found yourself unable to summon the suspension of disbelief required to imagine what Moran'd'arth actually looks like, well, then...you'll be in for a treat. But for now, baby steps.

Lastly, I'd like to touch on what's next for me, if for no other reason than to paint myself into such an embarrassingly specific corner that I can't get out of it. The next major project I work on will contain elements from the plots of *The Vampire and the Dragon* (most of my peers came to know me because of that aborted Inkshares attempt) and *PrOOF (Preservation Of Occult Figures)* which are basically the same story when you get right down to it. The main characters will be a vampire, a djinn, and the goddess Kali. If you read "Peta Babkama Luruba" from *ENANTIO-DROMIA*, then you already know the origin of the djinn in question.

This novel – tentatively titled *A History of Blood* – will delve into themes such as strength of will, mortality, and destiny. It will heavily feature blood magic and some sensuality. I can't wait for you to read it. Once I actually figure out how to write it, that is.

Until then, keep reading – especially indie authors, because we're trying to pay our rent...not the mortgages on our summer homes – and please never stop embracing me.

Michael James Welch
12/4/23

P.S. The safe word is "Platypus."

Trigger warnings:

The death of a child; a brief instance of underage prostitution; slavery; infidelity; alcoholism and alcohol consumption; a brief reference to an active shooter situation; IV drug use & overdose from same; brief reference to suicide; a spider; murder; heretical depictions of deities; strong language and some sexual situations throughout.

CONTENTS

TURNING OF THE BONES

 The dying person cannot wait for the shroud to be woven.

— MALAGASY PROVERB

When I was eight years old, my father started taking me for a walk each weekend. Our circuit was a rough circle around our hometown of Anjiro, and every week that circle expanded. This was his way of showing me how much there was outside of our small house in a small village without me losing my sense of center. If he had simply told me we were going on a long hike to the city of Antananarivo, then I would have only registered the departure point and the destination. Taking these ever-widening routes allowed me to keep one eye on home and the other on Madagascar at large. When I became a father myself, I realized all of these things. As a child, I was just happy to have my father's undivided attention. He took the opportunity most weekends to teach me about Malagasy culture, something he felt was slipping away from the youth of our country.

One weekend, my father introduced me to the *famadihana*.

It was 1930 and the Great War had been over for more than a decade. Madagascar was still chafing against the French colonizers, but things were

1

calm and happy for the most part. That weekend, in Anjiro, the town was filled with music, with voices singing and shouting. The smell of roasting meat hung in the air. The village elders had selected a fattened pig to be slaughtered for the event, and it seemed as though half of Anjiro was gathered around the fire pit, salivating.

Near the cemetery, dozens of people danced. Men I had seen sitting stationary in town all my life were blowing into trumpets, beating on drums with wooden sticks, and slapping tambourines against their skinny hips. I had not known them capable of movement until then. Every man wore a hat, and every woman's hair was elaborately braided. My father and I perched on a nearby hill and watched. Whenever I turned my face up to him in question, he would simply smile and direct me to watch the celebration. I saw many families crouched on the ground around white columns of cloth. I saw even more families that were carrying these columns on their shoulders – one family member for each end of it! Invariably, they were all dancing.

Once he was confident that I had absorbed the spectacle, he drew me away gently and we walked together until the sound of the *famadihana* faded in the distance.

"You have questions." He phrased this as a statement.

"Yes, Father."

With a sly raise of his eyebrow, he encouraged me to continue.

"What were those white bundles?" My young voice conveyed confusion and the slightest bit of dread. I knew in my heart what they were, but the idea of a dead body still frightened me.

"Those were the ancestors of the people holding them."

"Their grandfathers?"

He nodded, smiling.

"Why were they dancing? It was like a party."

He nodded again, doffed his hat briefly to wipe his brow, then stopped and faced me. "Malagasy honor their ancestors, Tombo. We unwrap the bodies from the old *lamba* cloth and place them in new, fresh *lamba*. We write their names on the cloth so that no one becomes confused as to who is who. We dance with them because we rejoice in the good fortune that they have helped to bring us. What you could not hear over the music was those people telling their ancestors about all the things that had happened since the last *famadihana* – the marriages, the births, and yes, even the deaths. They are still a part of their families, these departed, you see?"

I nodded, squinting against the midday sun peeking around the brim of his hat.

"It is a happy time," he continued. "Death is not always the end."

I did not know what to make of that, so I asked, "Do you want me to carry you around and sing and dance after you die?"

My father burst out laughing at this, which was rare. He was a pleasant man, but he was rarely given to big reactions. "Oh, Tombo, I *insist* on it!"

He turned and resumed walking, and after a short moment of thought, I ran to catch up with him. I put my hand in his and we walked for a while in silence again.

We stopped for a drink from the canteen that he had been given in the army – something that he always seemed to carry with him, now – and he looked at me. We sat with the sun at our backs, warm but not as hot as it was earlier. Without me pressing him, he asked me if I understood the *famadihana* now that he had explained it. I must have worn confusion on my face, because he began telling me the story of the origin of the *famadihana*.

"*Zanahary*, who, as you know, created the sky, found himself in a creative mood one day. *Zanahary* was always creating things, which is why there are so many stars in the sky. So on this day, he created the spirit of man." He touched his finger to his heart, then to his forehead. "The soul of man which makes each person truly unique.

"Now *Zanahary* usually left things up in the heavens, because that was his domain. But he could see that these spirits were not going to be happy just floating around up there. It seemed to *Zanahary* that they begged to be made alive...just like all the animals that roamed the earth and swam the seas.

"So *Zanahary* went to his half-brother *Ratovantany* and made a bargain with him. *Ratovantany* is the one who created the earth and everything on it; the animals, the water, the plants – everything that touches the ground. The bargain *Zanahary* made was this: he asked *Ratovantany* to allow these spirits of man to have bodies which would walk upon the earth. In exchange, when each man's time on earth was done, *Ratovan-*

3

tany could keep the bodies he had created, and the spirits would ascend back to *Zanahary*.

"At first, *Ratovantany* was reluctant. He told his half-brother that there were already so many animals on earth, that the seas were deep and wide but still packed with so many fish that no god could see to the bottom! *Zanahary* knew his brother was a prideful god, though, and told him that he would share man's worship with him, that they would both be gods to these new beings. *Ratovantany* thought about this and finally agreed, for there are no gods in the universe who do not crave more worship.

"*Ratovantany* started to create bodies for the men. *Zanahary* was shocked at how many different kinds of bodies his brother could come up with! There were bodies for men and for women, there were thin ones and fat ones. There were dark ones and light ones, tall ones and little baby ones! Right away *Zanahary* started hurling the spirits down into the bodies, and he saw very quickly that they were walking and talking and dancing and making love and so very, very happy to have been made alive. *Zanahary* smiled to himself and rested and watched his creations spread across the world.

"After some time, the trickster god *Mahaka* went to his cousin, who was called *Kotofetsy*, and told him he was bored. He complained that they had not come up with a really good trick in some time, not since the time they had made the waters rise. *Kotofetsy* thought on this and agreed, and together they set about coming up with a really good trick to play.

"Finally, *Kotofetsy* had an idea. He called to *Mahaka* and whispered in his cousin's ear a plan to pit the two gods – *Zanahary* and *Ratovantany* – against each other. They considered this great fun, these two tricksters, devising complicated plans that would vex the other gods. The idea was this: *Mahaka* would go to one end of Madagascar and *Kotofetsy* the other, and they would whisper in the ears of man a new idea. The trickster gods lied to the people and told them that mankind was nameless and faceless to the gods *Zanahary* and *Ratovantany*, and that it would please *Mahaka* and *Kotofetsy* to have mankind hide the dead bodies in anonymous graves, wrapped in *lamba*. As a reward, *Mahaka* and *Kotofetsy* would teach mankind new music.

"Now, what the tricksters actually did was learn music from each end

4

of the island and then take that music to the *other* end and teach it to the people there, and the people could not tell because they had truly never heard this music before! And so man began burying the dead in unmarked graves and tombs, wrapped in plain, white *lamba*, with no markings to distinguish one body from another.

"After some time, *Zanahary* realized that he was not getting his usual number of spirits back from earth. He sent his son, *Andrianerinerina*, down to speak to *Ratovantany* to see what the earth god was up to. *Ratovantany* was not happy to be accused of reneging on his bargain with *Zanahary*, and he demanded that a council of the gods be convened.

"Deep in the earth, the gods assembled. There were many there, but the main ones were *Zanahary, Ratovantany, Andrianerinerina, Mahaka, Kotofetsy*, and the first man who had ever been created, *Andriambahomanana*, to whom the moon had been given as a token of honor by *Zanahary*. They argued for days and nights on end; accusations flew and tempers rose. Just when it seemed like there would be a war between the heavens and the earth, *Andriambahomanana* – who sees what happens in both night *and* day – noticed that *Mahaka* and *Kotofetsy* were sitting quietly, covering their mouths and looking at each other with squinted eyes.

"The whole room stopped when the moon god stood and pointed at the two trickster gods. These two looked fully at each other and finally burst out, slapping their legs and nearly falling backward because they were laughing so hard. *Zanahary* and *Ratovantany* rose from the table and strode over to the tricksters, hauling them up by the collars of their tunics. The stern looks on the faces of the two creators sobered the tricksters right up, and they confessed their prank. In return, *Ratovantany* turned *Mahaka* into a spider and fixed him to the wall, while *Zanahary* threw *Kotofetsy* so far into the sky that he hasn't fallen back down to earth yet, to this very day.

"The gods took their seats and put their minds to how to fix this situation, as many years had passed on earth and man had grown accustomed to burying his dead anonymously. There was much discussion and disagreement, and it seemed that the two creator gods might again come to blows over this problem.

"Finally, *Zanahary*'s son, *Andrianerinerina*, came up with a solution.

He would appear to man and tell them they had been deceived, and that a compromise had been reached among the gods. Man would still wrap his dead in *lamba* cloth, but he should write the name of the dead upon the cloth, so that *Ratovantany* could see whose body he was taking back into the earth. Man should, every few years, bring their dead back out from the ground, or from the rocky caves and tombs, and unwrap the *lamba* cloth. This would allow the spirits the chance to return to heaven if they chose to. And they could wrap the bodies back in new *lamba*, with their names written on it anew, and place them back in their tombs and graves. This way, everyone got what they wanted.

"*Zanahary* beamed with pride at the wisdom of his son, and even *Ratovantany* smiled and embraced the young god in appreciation. *Zanahary* and *Ratovantany* nodded to each other, signaling that they were no longer angry, and the gods dispersed, leaving *Mahaka* in the dark, cold corner of the cave they held their meeting in.

"And so *Andrianerinerina* went to all the kings and chiefs of man and told them of the *famadihana*, and that it was to be held once every five years, and that it was to be a celebration of man's return to family, to the earth, and to the heavens. And that is why there is music and dancing and wonderful food at the 'turning of the bones' every five years, my son."

I sat stunned at his telling of this tale. My mouth hung open.

"What do you think, Tombovelo?" he asked gently.

"Is..." I hesitated briefly, worried my question might be an accusation. "Is that true, Papa?"

He smiled, understanding at once my hesitation. "That is how my father told it to me, Tombo, and how his father told *him*, and back and back and back."

I thought for a moment longer, and during this time my father stood and began gathering his things – the hat he had set down next to him while he spoke, his omnipresent canteen. "Papa?"

He turned back to me with a patient expression on his face, despite his body language showing that he was ready to walk again.

"What happens if the family does not do the...*famad*...the 'turning of the bones?'

For the first time that day, his face darkened. "Nothing good, my son. Nothing good."

6

IT IS OCTOBER OF 1942, and my father is fighting in the war which spilled over into Madagascar six short months ago. Nothing much has changed for us since Hitler came to power in Europe; our repressive colonizers were French then and they are still French now. They have a new name, but this makes little difference to most Malagasy, even if these *Vichy French* are considerably fonder of fascism than their predecessors.

Given his past as a soldier, my father has been conscripted into the defense of the island. A British invasion started in Diego-Suarez and has gradually bled south and west toward Antananarivo to capture the pesky Armand Annet, the staunchly pro-Vichy governor of our island. The irony of Malagasy being tasked with risking their lives to defend a fascist coward is not lost on many.

My mother has taken to spending most of her days with my wife, Finoana, and I in our small home since my father deployed earlier this year. Finoana is pregnant again. My son Rakoto is a toddler and cries often, and we are glad for the help of my mother.

There is a knock on the door in the early afternoon. I open the door to find a wiry, open-shirted Malagasy man whose face features a massive scar running from his temple to the corner of his mouth on the left side. It does not make him ugly so much as frightening. I find no words will come.

"Tombovelo, I am Tanjona!" Tanjona thrusts his hand out, and when I still do not move, grasps my right hand with his own and shakes it in greeting. His manner softens ever so subtly. "Tombo, I fought beside your father."

"Tanjona." I repeat his name respectfully. I do recall my father mentioning this man's name. What I remember is that my father trusted him, but also considered him crazy. I decide to trust him as well.

"Tombovelo, I have grave news." Tanjona's eyes look at his feet, and for the first time, I can see that there is a cart outside. Before he can continue, and before I can ask, my mother arrives behind me. She takes one look at Tanjona, then surges past both of us out into the street and immediately begins wailing at the sight of what is in the cart.

7

It is my father's body, covered partially with a blanket. His bootless feet stick out from the far end.

Tanjona looks up at me now, his eyes searching for forgiveness. Despite the grief settling on me, I take his hand again and let him know, silently, that he has brought us great relief by returning our father's body to Anjiro. I go past him and grip my mother by her shoulders. She is kneeling by the cart, shaking and repeating my father's name like a prayer. Finoana appears in the doorway with a wailing Rakoto in her arms, and Tanjona takes a few awkward steps backward into the street.

I look up at Tanjona again, intending to voice my thanks and give him the chance to leave if he would like. Before I can say anything, he quietly says, "I will be up the street, drinking," and turns on his heel. I continue to console my mother.

AFTER DINNER, when my mother has calmed down, I steal out of the house and head to where I suspect Tanjona has gone. There is a home further up the street that serves as an unofficial "pub" for our town. I have never set foot in it, but, like most people in Anjiro, I know of it.

Inside, I find Tanjona at a rickety table staring into his glass of liquor. There is a bartender, but he appears to be snoozing under the brim of his hat. I sit across from Tanjona.

Tanjona reaches over and grips my forearm in greeting. The man is clearly drunk, but to what degree, I have no idea. He smiles at me, his eyes half-lidded.

"Thank you, Tanjona, for bringing my father home."

Tanjona nods his head. He seems ready to speak, but unsure of what to say.

'How long did you know my father, Tanjona?"

"Oh, that is a story, my boy," Tanjona answers, his voice crisp. He raises his eyebrows as if to ask *are you sure you want to hear the whole thing?* and when I do not answer, he continues. "I first met Herv – your *father*," he corrects himself dramatically, "back at the beginning of '18. We were both recruited by the *French*–" Tanjona's voice drips with derision– "for the Kaiser's War."

"How did you get to know each other, though?" I prodded.

Tanjona smiles at this, clearly reliving the memory. "Ah, Tombovelo, let's just say that your father was very, *very* good at getting me out of scrapes. Every time I found myself in trouble – in the mess hall, on leave in town, in Diego Suarez proper, anywhere I went – your father was always there to help me out of it. He was a smooth one, your father."

I think about this description, and it matches what I know of my father's personality. He wasn't one for big displays of emotion. He was the kind of man who would rarely raise his voice. But I had the impression that whenever he did raise it, everyone would stop what they were doing and listen. Tanjona being the playful one to my father's stoic caretaker made sense. After a long pause, I speak again. "My father never told me why he joined the army. Why did you join?"

"Why did I join?" Tanjona repeats to himself, rolling his eyes slightly and taking another swig of the dwindling liquid. "If you wanted citizenship with the *French*–" again, the disdain wells off of Tanjona– "you had to be one of their *tirailleurs*. If you wanted to have any chance of escaping the rice paddy, you had to be one of their *tirailleurs*. If you wanted anything –" His voice rises, then trails off.

Tanjona knows how bitter he sounds and knows it will do no good to show me. His knee starts bouncing with agitation then.

I nod to him in understanding. That my father had returned to farming – both in rice paddies and on plantations – was known to both of us. My father never said anything against farming; indeed, he always indicated to me that it was an honor "to work in the richest soil on this Earth, Madagascar's."

"Do not mistake me, Tombo, farming is an honorable way to make a living," Tanjona seems to have read my thoughts. "It is simply that – well, the Malagasy do not own the farms, you see? We are not the boss – will never be the boss – and so the pay is bad, the work is hard and long, and so on. You see?"

I wave my hand lightly to indicate that I have not taken offense. The only money I have ever earned has been through taking jobs picking crops. I have not yet found a steady job to support my family.

Tanjona continues. "Your father and I went through basic training together. The French recruited tens of thousands of us to go to Europe and die in their trenches, did you know that?" He does not wait for a reply. "And those who did not die at the ends of German guns died of typhus or influenza. Your father and I barely missed being shipped over to Europe. The war ended a week before we were scheduled to leave."

I raise my eyebrows at this. My father never told me how close he had come to being in the war. He would never have mentioned the fact that he would not have made it back alive. "Did my father ever tell you why he joined?" I ask quietly.

Tanjona smiles. "He hinted about meeting a girl – your mother. They were so young – we were fifteen when we joined up. He wanted to be able to support her and start a family. He knew, even at that age, that she was the one for him."

We sit in silence for a few minutes. Tanjona once again studies his glass of liquor – nearly empty – for answers that will not likely come. I think of five years from now and the *famadihana* that my father wished for. "Tanjona, may I ask you something?"

Tanjona's raises his head, a devilish smile spreads across his face. "Anything, young Tombovelo."

"What do you think happens after we die?"

Tanjona's thin eyes mist a little at this question, and he shakes his head slowly from side to side before answering, "I don't think anything happens. There is just black, and sleep."

"So you do not hold to the *famadihana*, or to the possibility of Heaven? Or of becoming *angatra*?"

Tanjona's smile disappears, but his face remains passive, his half-lidded eyes still moist. "I think it is important to the dead what *they* believe," he says. "I think if you die an old man, at home in your bed, surrounded by your family, that you might certainly go to what feels like Heaven. Or if you die angry, or by violence..." Tanjona holds this thought a bit longer than he seems comfortable with, then seems to lose patience with the discussion. "I think you can make your own life – and death – a Hell if you try hard enough, Tombovelo. There are plenty of people walking around this island who you might call ghostly *angatra* already."

THE NEXT DAY we wrap my father's body in fresh *lamba* and place it in our family crypt on the outskirts of town. I see Tanjona walk by while I write my father's name on the cloth, but he does not speak to my mother or stay to meet the family formally. After the short ceremony, I excuse myself from my family and track Tanjona down at the bar again. Today, the place has more people in it, and Tanjona is less melancholy. Again, I sit across from him at the table. This time, he has procured an entire bottle. We pick up almost immediately where we left off last night, when I asked Tanjona about the *famadihana*.

"Tombo, your father was a happy man when he died." Tanjona nods in assent to his own statement. "We were waiting in ambush for the British, we held weapons and there was the occasional plane running sorties over our heads, but we had no fear. We knew the British were hunting for that idiot of a governor, Annet, and there were few of our company willing to fight for that man."

I say nothing, but I smile at Tanjona lightly.

Tanjona continues. "The last conversation your father and I had, he was telling me how happy he was that things seemed to be winding down. We knew Annet was running out of places to hide. We knew they would find him soon, and then we could all stop pretending to be Vichy. In fact, your father and I were next to each other talking about how we could work together to put an awning over your front door when he was hit by the bullet. The British managed to ambush us while we were trying to do the same to them, and some fool shot at them. The Brits returned fire, briefly. It was over in a minute, and I looked down and there was your father, slumped forward against the sandbags we had filled the day before. I called his name, but he didn't answer. I pulled back on his shoulder and saw that he was hit in the chest. And that was that, Tombovelo."

I bow my head. Part of me is happy that my father did not suffer, but the bitterness is rising at the colonizers who put him in that position in the first place.

I look up at Tanjona. I yearn to take the burden of my father from him completely; he should let go and know that he has done a great service to our family. Understanding passes between us wordlessly, and Tanjona nods once at me.

Looking to lighten the mood, Tanjona raises his voice and asks me, loudly, "What's that, you say, Tombovelo? You want to know how I got this scar?" A few others in the pub look his way, hoping to overhear the tale themselves.

I laugh. "Sure, why not tell me, Tanjona?"

He grins. "Where to start? This was back in 'thirty-two. Two of my friends and I had been drinking wine all day – terrible, homemade stuff. André finished puking his guts up in an alley behind some building, and we all realized it was a tavern. It was not the kind we normally went into; it looked like it served a very specific type of customer – the French. I cannot remember the name of the place if I ever even knew it at all.

"We walked in and, of course, every single person in the bar turned and glared at us. We were already drunk enough not to care, but then Henri – my other friend – realized that he knew the bartender. All the wait staff were Malagasy, as you might have guessed. Henri went up to the bar with me and André behind him. Henri's friend – I could never remember his name – was wide-eyed and starting to sweat. Henri reached out to shake his hand, and his friend didn't take it. The friend hissed something like *what do you want?* and of course we took that as the cue to put in our drink orders. Looking back, I do not think that is what he meant when he asked. There was a long period of staring over the bar among the four of us, and then the bartender relented and got our orders. Most of the bar patrons had resumed their conversations or gazing at their drinks or whatever it was they were doing before we walked in.

"Not all, of course. Three uniformed French soldiers occupied a table in the very back corner, and their attention was fully on us. Why they were in full uniform during peacetime we never understood. Maybe it had to do with the incursions rebels were making against them. I had not yet taken up arms against them, personally, but some Malagasy had. So that was probably it.

"Henri's bartender friend came back with our drinks – two pale lagers for them and an absinthe for me. He held out his hand, expecting payment, and Henri started to babble excuses at him while André and I left the bar. We took the only open table, which was fortunately as far away from the soldiers as possible.

"Another round of staring from all the white, French patrons started when we sat down. Henri finally disengaged from his friend – who was enraged based on the look consuming his face – and sat with us at the table. For whatever reason, his arrival eased the other customers' nerves enough for them to mind their own business again.

"André began to ask Henri what his friend's problem was, but Henri shook his head as if to say *leave it alone*. My companions drank their lagers in quiet, and I sipped my absinthe. We engaged in hushed conversation among ourselves, the topic of which I do not recall. It does not matter anyway. All of us were occupied with chasing this woman or that woman; none of us were married. We might have had some kids.

"Anyway, I occupied the seat that was furthest in the corner and therefore had a full view of the bar. André was to my left, and Henri had taken the seat that put his back fully to the bar. Personally, I think that was for the best, because his bartender friend kept staring at the back of Henri's head while we drank. If looks could have killed…

"We were about done with our drinks – I had just tossed back the last of my absinthe – when I noticed that all three soldiers were standing at the end of the bar speaking to Henri's friend. The same end that we had ordered from. So they were pretty close to us now. The bartender looked terrified. One of the soldiers ignored their conversation completely and just stared straight over at us. Henri and André saw me looking back toward the bar, and both slowly turned. At that moment, our eyes were locked on the three soldiers and the hapless bartender who was holding his hands out as if to say *I did not ask them to come here!*

"And their eyes were locked on us.

"It might have been the absinthe – which, by the way, Tombo, you should never, ever drink – but at that moment, my temper came up. I stood up from my chair, still staring at the soldiers. All of them raised their eyebrows at this, perhaps thinking they were about to have some good sport with some of the locals. The bartender started protesting even louder then. One of the soldiers – the big one that I ended up dancing with – put their palm fully on the bartender's face and pushed him backward. He fell out of our view.

"At the thud made by the bartender's fall, both Henri and André were immediately on their feet. My soldier – clearly the leader of the trio – advanced on our table. Henri moved closer to my right. André looked like he might vomit again. They told me later that I was smiling at the soldiers. A humorless smile.

"The soldier asked us – in French, of course – what we were doing there. I replied that we were enjoying a drink. None of them seemed to find that funny, because each of their mouths became stern, straight lines. He asked why were weren't enjoying it with our own *kind*. I asked him what *kind* he was referring to – French-speaking drunks?

"Now the soldier's smile was back, but it was a humorless grimace, like mine. It did not reach his eyes, you know? He changed tactics and asked me if I knew any of the recent participants in a protest against French rule in the city – one that had turned violent and led to more than a few fires being set in the streets. I told him that I had no idea what he was talking about, but if it was such a problem for the Malagasy to speak their minds, then maybe the French should simply leave.

"That was it. All the smiles on the soldiers' faces fell off right then.

"Henri practically leapt into my arms to avoid the table as the soldier swept it to his left with one arm. Our glasses shattered against the wall, but the table, upended as it was against the wall, shielded us from any broken glass. André threw a punch in the direction of the first soldier, but he dodged it easily and used the momentum of Andre's swing to pass him to his comrades behind him. Henri – always a lover and not a fighter – made the mistake of trying to evade both me and the soldier to get to the door, but he was similarly swung into the arms of the third soldier.

"I turned my back on the soldier advancing on me to grasp the back of my chair, then swung it fully into the side of his head. Apparently he had not expected this, because it connected fully and sent him sprawling into the corner, behind the overturned table. I took a run at the soldier manhandling André, lowering my shoulder into his ribs and sending him sideways into the bar. His head connected with the bar rail, and he sank to the floor.

"With this moment's reprieve, I glanced around the bar and saw that the patrons – none of whom seemed heroic in the least – had stood from their tables and were cowering in the back of the room, as far away from the carnage as possible. Henri made some sort of strangled noise behind me. I spun deftly and planted my fist directly in the remaining soldier's nose, breaking it and sending blood spurting into the humid air.

"With our three assailants down, Henri, André and I shared amused looks and headed for the door. Henri's friend was once again standing behind the bar, waving his hands and babbling in a confused mixture of French and Malagasy. My two friends made it out the door, but the first soldier grabbed me on the right shoulder. He was certainly one tough customer, because I looked right at him and saw where the chair leg had dented his skull, close to his right temple. What I did not see, however, was the massive knife he had drawn in his right hand.

"He swept it up at an angle so quickly that I only saved my eye by falling backward. My face felt warm and wet, the pain only lasting a moment. The soldier regained his bearings after his wild swipe and advanced on me. I was on my back, the light was coming in through the door to my left, and the gasps of the crowd to my distant right were quieting. I drew back my right leg and aimed my heel at the soldier's crotch, then thrust with all my might. I know that I hit something, but I never waited to find out what or where. I scrambled to my feet, slipping at first in my own blood, and launched myself through the door and into the street.

"By now, all the commotion had drawn people from the businesses nearby. They began to congregate outside of the tavern and were looking back and forth between the front door and the cluster of we bloodied three friends. Henri took one look at my face and turned nearly white. André implored me to move faster, pointing me away from the tavern and out of sight as much as he could. I was half turned around, looking over my right shoulder for pursuit from the soldiers. The only – and last – thing I saw for the rest of that day was Henri's bartender friend being pushed roughly out into the street, where he stood rigidly complaining that this *was not his fault*. Then there was a loud bang and a puff of smoke from the doorway, and Henri's friend went down like a felled tree. As Henri and André lifted my arms over their shoulders and started running, I heard all manner of screams and shouts fading behind us."

I am left speechless by Tanjona's tale, both at the brutality of the French and the violence Tanjona is capable of. The other bar patrons, however, are celebrating the man as if he were a war hero. I shake his hand and make my way out of the pub, which is threatening to devolve into a chorus of songs from the First World War. On the short walk home, I feel as though I have just escaped from something. I avoid the pub from then on.

———

IN NOVEMBER OF 1945, my mother joins my father in the family crypt. She goes quickly and quietly from what is probably cancer, but none of us can afford to pay for an autopsy. It hardly matters, as she lived longer than any of her ancestors. The mid-40s seem to be the best most of us can hope for.

The Vichy regime has been replaced by free French. Despite having just lived directly under crushing fascism, most of the newly arrived French seem on edge. Protests against French rule have intensified, particularly in the major cities of Madagascar. French patrols pass through Anjiro on their way west to Antananarivo regularly, but none are interfered with. Our village elders have cautioned us against bringing down any colonial wrath on our heads. After they make these claims, their eyes dip in shame. They are the last generation to have been born in a free Madagascar. One would think that they would be the thirstiest for freedom, but it is apparently not so.

The rebel actions against the French are becoming more brazen. The rumors of what the French are doing in reprisal are becoming more horrific. There are tales of roadside executions. Of men being dropped hundreds of feet from helicopters to their deaths. Stories of all manner of extrajudicial killings make the rounds from village to village. Some pass these off as French propaganda, told only to scare us into accord. Others insist on having known some of the victims and swear that these terrible acts are truly happening on our island. Divisiveness is the order of the day. While the rest of the world celebrates freedom from tyranny, Madagascar languishes. Anger toward these colonizers grows in my heart.

———

IT IS August of 1947 and the air is starting to cool considerably. It has been a very dry season, and the farms have not needed as much help; many young men are unemployed. I am outside of my home, sitting in front of my door, facing west with my eyes closed. My skin soaks up the fleeting warmth of the setting sun. Two men pass by on the road, and I sense them stop.

"No. I am telling you, no," one of them says, and his voice is familiar.

The other man is not convinced, and tells his companion that he doesn't care, and that he is going to talk to me. I open my eyes.

I see Tanjona standing out in the road with his hands posted impatiently on his hips.

"Young man." The other steps into my line of sight and holds out his hand for me to shake. "I am Aristide. I want to talk to you about our country."

I take the man's hand and shake it firmly, but we forgo the traditional kisses on the cheek.

Tanjona materializes next to Aristide, scowling. "Tombovelo," is all he says.

"Tanjona," I say, smiling at him. Regardless of his mood, I am happy to see him again. I turn my gaze to the other man. "Hello, Aristide. How can I help?"

Aristide turns to Tanjona and smiles broadly. "You see, Tanjona? This one is more than happy to talk to us about freedom!" Aristide turns to me. "The world war is over, Tombo, but Madagascar is not free. The French have their heel on the throat of our freedom!"

Tanjona's face betrays barely concealed rage. He grasps Aristide's forearm and hisses, "I served with Tombovelo's father. I brought his body home." Tanjona waits a moment to let the gravity of his words sink in. "He is no soldier."

Barely missing a beat, Aristide replies to Tanjona while smiling at me. "So many of the brave rebels taking up arms against the colonizers are not soldiers!" He gently pulls his forearm free from Tanjona and faces me squarely. "Have you been working, son?"

Aristide knows I have not been. Barely anyone in Anjiro has worked in the last three months. I do not answer him. In fact, I speak directly to Tanjona. "A rebellion? An organized one?"

For years now, isolated attacks against French interests on our island have been happening. Every so often, a man from Anjiro will be taken by

French officials and never seen again. No explanation is ever given as to what the man did; he simply disappears.

Tanjona considers his answer, then nods curtly. He senses that this battle may already have been lost.

Aristide attempts to regain control of the conversation. "Tombo," he begins. Both Tanjona and I look at him, and he realizes that his ploy of familiarity is starting to wear out. "Tombovelo, yes, we are organizing a revolution against our French occupiers. There. Now you know enough to have Tanjona and me executed, if you like."

I wave his concern away with one hand. "Why do you want me to avoid this fight, Tanjona? I know how much you hate the French. Remember what you told me five years ago? That *we Malagasy would never own the farms, but always work them.*"

Tanjona looks down at his feet. "How can I let you fight if I promised your father I would look after you?"

My face softens at this, but what the man is saying is ludicrous. He has never put food on my table nor saved my life. He has not been some guardian angel. "Tanjona, you did right by my father when you brought his body home. You owe him nothing more. If you let me come fight for our independence from the French, you will help to ensure *my* future. How much better could you help my family than that?"

Aristide looks from my face to Tanjona's but has the good sense to keep his mouth shut.

Tanjona, still studying his feet, nods.

"In one month, come to the east of Tana," he says, using the colonial name for Antananarivo, "in the Betongolo neighborhood. We will find you."

I shake Aristide's proffered hand. Tanjona is looking at me darkly. I know he is not angry with me, only troubled. I nod to him respectfully.

"Bring a spear," Tanjona says, then turns and storms down the road without waiting for Aristide.

THAT EVENING, Finoana and I argue bitterly about my decision. She reminds me that when the French come to punish the rebels, it is the women and children that they hurt, not the men. "The man is hiding out in the jungle, carrying on with his friends," she chides.

I am holding my daughter, Mikanto, who is crying at our raised voices. I am trying to comfort her. Rakoto is watching us but stays silent, his six-year-old mind trying to accept the idea of becoming the man of the house once I depart.

I tell Finoana that nothing will happen to me, and that I will come home to her safely when Madagascar is free. She simply retrieves a few sheets of paper and a pencil and places them on the table before me. She stops Mikanto from grasping the pencil, which results in another round of wailing from the girl. Finoana stoops and takes my daughter from my arms, then straightens and looks down at me while bouncing Mikanto on her hip.

"Write me a letter. Tell me that you have gone to the south of the island to work the fields there. That way, when the French come to our door, *I* can save our family while you are out saving the country."

It is not the last conversation we have before I depart for Antananarivo three weeks later, but it is the last one we have about me leaving.

I write the letter.

In September of 1947, I perform the *famadihana* for my father's body. Finoana helps me wrap his desiccated corpse in the new *lamba* and works to sew the cloth shut while I write his name on the side with a charcoal pencil. I tell him that I am going to fight for Madagascar's freedom, and I ask for his guidance and protection. I barely need her help in carrying him on my shoulder, his body is now so light.

The next morning, I depart for the eastern suburbs of Antananarivo.

BY OCTOBER OF 1947, I am northwest of Manjakandriana watching a young French soldier die. His drab, olive uniform is spotted with dark maroon dots, and his beret has fallen from his head. He is lying on the forest floor, his blood soaking into my country. In the canopy, the lemurs are screeching.

The soldier had the misfortune of becoming separated from the rest of his unit and was wandering through the thick forest when we happened upon him. I was closest to where he stopped, and so it was my spear that pierced his neck. My cell – comprised of seven other rebels – moves on while the soldier still spasms on the ground. They fear the French unit doubling back to find their missing man. I linger, fascinated.

The forest smells stale and vibrant all at once. The plants decay on the ground, feeding the life abounding everywhere. The sharp tang of the soldier's panicked sweat cuts through the musk. I try to imagine how the boy feels about dying so far away from home, with no family to take care of his bones. I squat in a close thicket and watch him choke to death on his own blood. His eyes ask me for help, but I give none. Once he is still, I take his rifle and ammunition.

A month later, I am fighting on the rural outskirts of Antananarivo. My comrades and I have a group of French soldiers pinned in a small gully, having ambushed them during their afternoon meal. Many of my fellows hurl rocks down upon them, ranging from head-sized boulders to pebbles, with varying success. I am pointing my rifle at the group, so they have not gone for the rifles they left piled at our end of the gully. I check the bolt of the carbine rifle, ensure a round is chambered, and then fire a bullet into the temple of the only soldier foolish enough to go for their gun. His eyes lock on mine and go wide a moment before I pull the trigger. The report from the shot echoes across the farmland on which we fight.

After several long minutes, I see the French in the gully finally relax. They put their hands down, no longer having to defend against our projectiles. My fellows have stopped throwing rocks and have turned around, raising their hands. I am the last to turn, and I find a full regiment of angry French with rifles trained on us. I place my rifle on the ground and bring my hands up slowly. One of the soldiers fires anyway, and a pain jumps up and hits me in the head. All goes black and silent.

<Réveille ce morceau de merde!>

My French is rusty and my head won't clear. I am grabbed roughly by an elbow and thrust forward. My eyes fly open during my fall through a meter of fetid air.

It comes to me as my palms and knees strike dirt: *wake that piece of shit up.*

A shovel lands next to me with a clang and I pick it up without argument. I don't turn around to look at the Frenchman who threw both me and it into this pit. Instead, I look at my fellow soldiers. They are all bent to the task of deepening the pit we stand in. It stretches at least four meters across and two meters wide.

We are digging our own grave.

I see Tanjona stop digging, his lack of motion stark with the rest of us flinging the dark, rich soil of our beloved country over our shoulders. He is speaking, but I am too far away to hear. Tanjona turns and goes to the far edge of the pit, furthest from the French who are gathered in a loose circle, smoking cigarettes and laughing amongst themselves. He climbs out, turns to face them across the gulf of dirt, and thrusts his shovel defiantly to the ground. One of the French notices him and alerts his comrades.

<Reviens là-dedans!> the commandant shouts, gesturing into the pit with his chin. *Get back in there!*

Tanjona says nothing, but stands at the edge glaring at the French. His eyes are wild, and I can see a tremor in his left hand. We Malagasy have stopped digging and are staring at him.

The commandant unholsters his pistol and shouts, <À présent!> He gestures with the gun this time, flicking his wrist to indicate a return to the pit. *Now!*

Tanjona continues glaring, his eyes locked on the commandant's. He gives his head a subtle shake, and a smile creeps into a corner of his lip.

The commandant's pistol barks, causing us all to jump, even Tanjona. The man at the furthest end of the pit pitches forward into the dirt. Our eyes follow him down in confusion, but then we see the blood spurt from the wound in his back.

His name is Phillippe. He is not one of the rebels I am particularly close to.

Many things commence at once, now.

Tanjona stoops to pick up his shovel and turns away from the pit in one fluid motion, breaking into a full sprint. Phillippe twitches queerly on the ground, his eyes shocked and his mouth gawping like a fish out of water. Every French soldier who was seated is now on his feet. Those who never set down their rifles are sighting over the pit at Tanjona, who is holding the shovel over his shoulder to shield his back. The ones who had set theirs down snatch them up and alternate between aiming at Tanjona and jabbing them at the shocked men in the pit. We, in turn, stand in disarray; some watch the receding form of Tanjona, some flinch at the panicked Frenchmen suddenly thrusting rifle barrels in their faces. I am still watching Phillippe jerk. His eyes are flung wide; the right one is pressed into the ground. His breath disturbs the dirt near his open mouth. His heart pumps blood only to have it leak onto the ground. He is not dead yet but is clearly on the path.

Shots ring out from the French. There are several distant *clangs* as their slugs hit Tanjona's shovel. They are each shouting at Tanjona, <arrêter!> (*stop!*), but he is running at frantic angles and has evaded them for at least fifty meters. After another deafening volley, Tanjona goes down hard and does not move again.

My compatriots lift themselves up on the edge of their toes, hopeful for some sign of movement in the tall grass, but there is none. The French, similarly looking for any sign that Tanjona survived, are gradually lowering their rifles and exchanging satisfied smiles. My head rings with pain and the gun smoke invades my nose. I thrust the shovel blade into the dirt again.

A FEW HOURS AFTER, Phillippe is still, although his eyes remain wide. The sun has set and the French are discussing what to do—be done with us now or have us continue digging? Their concern is apparently that if it is not deep enough, this grave will be uncovered by animals within hours of their departure.

Further down the pit, Jean-Marc has given to sobbing quietly. The French told him to get back to digging once, but then gave up on the idea and just let him cry. The man closest to me – one I am barely acquainted with named Serge – is simmering with anger. He mutters to himself in a mixture of French and Malagasy, and his shovel's blade bites deep into the earth. I find myself distracted by the idea of my family not being able to find my body. Dying here is a foregone conclusion. No one besides the men in this pit knows where we are; there is no high command tracking our rebellious movements. How will Finoana ever find my body and place me in our family crypt in Anjiro?

For the first time since that day, I think of the young French soldier I watched die in the jungle.

A horrible smell pulls my thoughts back to the pit. Serge has squatted about two feet from me, his pants down around his ankles. He holds his hand under his hovering bottom. When he sees me looking his way, he flashes a devilish smile.

I know what is about to happen, but short of swinging my shovel at Serge's head, there is nothing I can do to stop it.

I have dropped my shovel and started backing away from Serge by the time his feces hits the closest French soldiers. A volley of curses is followed by the uniform raising of rifles. The commandant, somehow looking both haggard and wild-eyed, barks a command at his men: *don't shoot!*

The men turn to him in disbelief – how can he allow this to go unpunished? The soldiers who had been pinned in the gulley by our cell seem particularly agitated.

The commandant lowers himself clumsily into the pit, his grunt of effort stained with disgust at having to do so. He strides over to Serge, who by now has pulled his pants back up and is attempting to cinch his belt with his clean hand.

Serge does not notice that the commandant brought his rifle with him.

The commandant swings the butt of the rifle at Serge while he is looking down at his own waist. There is a terrible crack – whether it is the wood of the rifle or the bone of Serge's skull, I do not know. Serge goes down without breaking his own fall, rolls on to his back, and through confused eyes looks up at the commandant who now stands astride him.

After the commandant's third blow with the rifle butt to Serge's face, all the soldiers are now in the pit with us.

Since I am at the furthest edge of the pit, the soldiery descends on the rest of my compatriots first. It seems we are too tired to yell, because the only sounds I can hear are the rough connections of wood striking bone and the crunch of collapsing skulls. After a moment of standing over Serge's body, panting, the commandant seems to sense my presence and turns. His eyes betray no hint of sanity or control. He swings the rifle at me wildly and I find I am backed up against the earthen wall of the pit. The butt connects with my left forearm, held out defensively, and instantly breaks the bone. I drop to my side, my left hip on the floor of the pit. I'm unable to raise my right arm fast enough to defend against the next blow that connects with my head.

A shot rings out before the commandant can continue.

I make good on the commandant's distraction and lie prone on the ground, eyes closed. I have no doubt that my bleeding head and filthy body give a convincing impression of death. The commandant curses quietly in my direction before turning around and stalking to the middle of the pit. I hazard opening my eyes only a little, and I see that the French are now once again in a circle of discussion. Dead, stunned, and dying Malagasy men curl at their ankles. The French kick viciously at them if their boots are touched.

Next to me, Serge is moving his arms slowly back and forth; his elbows are on the ground, his wrists are utterly limp. He moves as if trapped in tar. His left ankle slowly turns his foot to point outward.

One of the French has climbed out of the pit and is handing long objects down to his comrades. I cannot tell what they are, as my head feels once again full of fog. The French appear to be creating spears.

Bayonets. They are bayonets.

I see Finoana's face now, smiling at me on the day of our wedding. I see Rakoto's round face as I bid him farewell to go fight in this rebellion. I hear myself tell him not to cry, and that I will return. His sister, Mikanto, stands behind him sniffling. I remember kissing them each on the forehead.

Father, how will my family find my body?

A French soldier is playfully sinking his bayonet into Serge's torso. Serge's hands try to fend it off, but their slow motion comes nowhere near the blade. The knife is in and out four or five times before he moves at all. Serge's head is misshapen, his face completely swollen. Another French soldier carefully maneuvers his bayonet above one of Serge's eyes, trying to determine where it resides in that puffy mound before dropping the rifle's full weight into the slit. Serge goes slack.

I must make some sort of grunt of grief, because both soldiers turn toward me. The commandant looms between them and says, <Je pensais

que celui-ci était déjà mort.> *I thought this one was already dead.* He pulls his pistol from its holster and levels it at me. The soldiers next to him take a reflexive step back. He fires a slug into my torso, and then all is black.

My eyes open just a little at the sound of Tanjona's body being dropped into the pit. His limbs flop against the rich black of our beloved Madagascan soil. His eyes are both open, and the eyeballs have rolled up like he's trying to see the top of his own head. My stomach has a warm, dull pain from the bullet wound. I can't feel my legs. I am tired to my core and close my eyes to sleep.

I regain consciousness again when a shovel-load of dirt hits my back. I cannot move. Since I am lying on my side, my view is of the entire pit. The men I have fought beside are all dead. Most are covered in dirt, but I can see some of their faces; their white, vacant eyes staring into forever. Kiady, Litasoa, Huberto – all of them dead. Another shovelful of dirt hits me, this time on my neck. Dirt is in my eyes. I cannot blink it away. I see dawn starting to light the sky. Dirt is in my mouth, and I can taste the soil of my country. I cannot spit it out. I am thinking of how our families will not find our bodies, that none of us will be taken to the crypts of our ancestors. The dirt hits me in an irregular but clustered rhythm. It is getting harder to hear anything. Soon, more dirt and weight are piled on top, and everything has gone dark. I can just barely hear the French soldiers talking and laughing in muffled tones. I can hear the heavy trucks moving about, feel the rumble in the earth all around me.

In time, everything is silent.

I can't breathe.

Father? How will they find me?

MY PAIN IS GONE. Everything is dark. I am so tired that I cannot move. I hear my voice being spoken. It is not the same as someone calling out to me; it is like they are mentioning my name in conversation. Every time they do, I can hear it. I still feel paralyzed, but there is no pain – just my inability to move. After a long time, everything goes silent. My name is no longer being spoken.

In the darkness and silence, fear blooms within me. Despite not feeling like I can move, I decide to do so. I rise above the surface of the earth, and the darkness is gone. I continue to rise slowly. I can see the mass grave from above now, and fear has left my heart. I decide to go into the forest, and instantly I am there. I decide to stand upon the ground, as a man would, and I am standing.

I can see but I cannot smell the forest nor feel Madagascar beneath my feet. I can hear if I concentrate on a sound; a warbling bird high on a limb calls out for a mate. The rain does not touch me, nor do the heat or cold. The sky flashes light and dark as days pass in seconds. I lift my face and call to *Zanahary*, who breathed life into all beings: *why have you not claimed me?* I look at the forest floor and call to *Ratovantany*, who claims the flesh of the dead: *why have you not released me?*

They do not answer me. I stand for many days and nights waiting. I am *angatra*, a ghost; life goes on around me but does not see me.

I decide to move west to my village, to Anjiro. The sky strobes with darkness and light, a day and night passing with every phantom stride I take. The trees and rocks are still; the roads, though they blur with the comings and goings of the living, lead me home.

I come to the doorstep of my house. This is a house I built with my father from mud brick; the roof is covered in gray thatched reeds but is strong. It has the luxury of not being too close to the houses on either side of it. The town has grown around it in my absence – there are houses in the neighborhood that were not here before. The door frame is still the light blue that I painted it, but it has faded. On the corrugated fiberglass awning, something I always wanted but could never afford, there is a set of wooden wind chimes. They hang motionless. I mouth the word "slow" and the sky ceases flashing.

A French soldier emerges from my house, cinching his belt. His brow is wet with sweat and I know, somehow, that he has been with a woman. Without even considering the action, I lash out with my hand. It passes through his cheek without touching him. He stops, though, as if he has heard something. I scream at him with all my strength, cursing him and his entire nation. He laughs at himself for hearing things, shakes his head, then moves on down the earthen street. My curses chase him.

I reach for the door of my home, but my hand passes through. Truly, I am a worthless ghost, unable to touch or feel or strike anything in the real world. On the threshold, I stand and despair. My wife is being used by French soldiers, and there is nothing I can do to stop it. The day turns to night, and gradually the sky resumes its rapid cycle.

I sense a shape close to me and will time to slow again. A French soldier is entering my house. I don't know – or care – if it's the same one or another of his kind. Without a second thought, I follow him through the open door.

He is speaking to a woman I don't immediately recognize. Random gray hairs speckle her brown hair. Her back is to us both, and she carries her body in a defeated pose, moving slowly. When she turns to receive a handful of clanking French franc coins from the soldier, I see that she is Finoana, my wife. She is much older than I remember, the wrinkles at her eyes more pronounced. Anger swells inside of me, and I have the sensation of growing; my perspective is from high in the corner of the kitchen, near the ceiling. Why is she selling her body? And of all the men on this island to sell it to – why these devils? Why isn't she searching for *my* body? How can our family perform the *famadihana*, the turning of the bones, if she has not found my body? There is no joy on either of their faces; her eyes are downturned and defeated, and his mouth is set in a grim, businesslike line.

"Don't lay with this scum, Fino!" I shout. "Use your time to find my body! I am *angatra*! *Angatra* because you are here with these bastards!" Deaf to my rage, the soldier heads into the hallway which leads to the bedrooms. Finoana sits down heavily at our kitchen table and covers her face in her hands. She is ashamed. I think, *good!*

Time passes and she does not get back up to meet with the soldier. Finoana's right leg bounces with anxiousness, and she continues to lean heavily into her left palm, her elbow on the table. Would that I could sweep my ethereal hand down and cause her elbow to move, to get her attention, anything. But she cannot, or does not, hear me. Confusion clouds my sight. I think of simply discovering where this bastard is, and instantly I am in the room with him and a young woman. They are having sex, the slapping of flesh and light squeaking of the bed springs is the only sound. The girl is on her back, with her head turned away and to the side. She does not appear to be distraught, but neither does she appear to be enjoying herself.

This is my daughter, Mikanto, I realize with mounting horror. Her head turns my way and I see her eyes – the same piercing, dark eyes my mother had. Her brow creases in light discomfort, and a frown flashes across her face. She cannot be more than sixteen. She was seven when I died. Somehow, almost ten years has passed since I died in that pit with my fellows. In that time, Finoana has sold Mikanto to the French army.

I feel myself growing, the room becoming smaller. I surpass the dimensions that Mikanto's dresser and bookshelves occupy. Blackness clouds the edge of my vision, and all I can see are the undulating muscles of this man's back. I lash out at the soldier as I did before, to his predecessor outside, not expecting any result. To my shock – and his – three long strips of flesh are flayed from his back. I can see his exposed muscles. Small dots of blood hit the paper of a crayon drawing taped beside Mikanto's bed. He screams and arches upwards in pain, his head thrown back. My daughter scrambles out from under his weight and tries to cover herself with a small pink pillow. The soldier turns to her in anger and raises his right arm as if to backhand her. He thinks she scratched him! She cowers in terror. Again, my rage spurts hot and I lower my shoulder into his side and charge like a bull. The soldier is thrown against the brick wall of her room. I wish to do more violence, for my form to grow and crush this devil against the wall, but I am suddenly very tired and cannot move. My mind fogs over. My daughter and her injured patron fade from my sight as the room becomes a blur. I am still standing over my daughter's bed, staring at the wall. Through the small, square window of her room, I watch day and night cycle by rapidly.

OVER TIME, I realize I am less tired, my head less foggy. I am still angry. My anger becomes anguish. My wife has sold our daughter as a whore. *Is this what I have made of my family?* I had sought to free my country from the grip of colonizers, and my reward is this? *What of my son, Rakoto? Where is he in all of this?*

By way of answer, I see a vision of Rakoto working in a distant field at the southeastern tip of my beloved island. He stops his work for a moment and looks up. He takes a small rag from his belt and wipes the sweat from his brow. He is facing west because the sun is in his eyes and causing him to squint. He is unhappy. I understand that he has taken this job to send money home to Finoana. He cannot be more than eighteen.

The heavy exhaustion descends on me again. My angst diminishes and my thoughts go blank. I do not see the room any longer. I simply stand and the world blurs around me, the days churning by through the small window.

I DO NOT KNOW how much time has passed when I hear my name spoken and the world slows again. I find myself outside rather than in my house. My body begins to ascend, and I see that I was standing in black-ened, burned ruins. The confusion causes me to want to stay, but I am compelled by the speaking of my name even more strongly. I am moving over the town, toward the cemetery. It is Rakoto and Mikanto who have said my name. I alight near them now.

They are wrapping a body in a long, white silken shroud of *lamba*. I concentrate and understand that it is my wife Finoana who has died. My children mourn for their mother. I look into their faces and see that they are older now than I was when I died. Mikanto has children by her side and her face is fixed with hatred. Rakoto turns to her and says that he does not believe that their father – me – became *angatra*. She shakes her head, scowling, lowers her eyes to the body of their mother and carefully lifts. Rakoto carries the other end of Finoana into our family crypt. My bones should rest beside hers in this crypt; if they did, I would not be this wandering spirit.

When Rakoto leaves the crypt, I trail him. He is staying in Antana-narivo, and I follow his car for many miles, effortlessly matching its speed. He arrives at a hotel in what appears to be a wealthy part of the city; certainly not a part I have ever stood in before. A uniformed man bows lightly to Rakoto and opens the door to the lobby for him. I follow Rakoto closely; if anyone could see me, they would think us attached. The lobby is dazzlingly bright, adorned with high ceilings and crystal-laden chandeliers. I follow my son to the massive brass doors of the elevator banks, and then into one of the elevators.

Finally, Rakoto arrives at a door on the fifth floor. He knocks at it gently, and a dark- skinned African woman answers, immediately letting him in. Her hair is short and closely cropped to her small, round head. Her cheekbones are high and her brown eyes large. Her beautiful face lights up when she sees my son. I slip in behind Rakoto before the heavy door shuts with a loud *clunk*. Rakoto hugs this woman, kisses her cheek, and tells her he's going to take a shower. She sits at a small table centered on the room's massive floor to ceiling windows. She looks at her vibrantly colored fingernails. She crosses and uncrosses her legs.

I wait.

Rakoto returns, dressed in a white bathrobe. The steam from his quick shower pursues him into the main part of the room. He sits at the small table, holding the hand of this woman – perhaps his wife? She asks him how it went. He answers that there was some problem with his sister. I move closer to them, worried that my presence might be felt, but they do not indicate that I am sensed. They have a quiet, intimate way about them, and I am grateful that my son, at least, seems to have found a better life than that of his sister.

"She insists that Father still haunts the house, or what's left of it," he says.

The woman frowns lightly, in pity for Mikanto, I realize. "She has had a hard life. This is the house that was burned down?"

Rakoto nods. "Mother said it was the French who torched it." Anger passes over his face briefly. "Mikanto swears that one time, when she was a teen, when times were...a lot harder..."

He looks down at his lap. "She was with a soldier, and something scratched that man's back. Three huge slashes. And since there was no one else in the room, he was going to hit Mikanto, and she says that she saw our father...or, something in the shape of our father...ram this man into the wall to stop him. She says that it looked like the outline of our father, but with red eyes, and long claws for fingers."

The woman looks aghast.

"Three long claws," Rakoto finishes.

My attention fades from their conversation briefly. I hear the word "*kinoly*" and I remember that this refers to a particularly rageful ghost who kills those with whom it is angry or displeased.

I am *kinoly*. I could not be more cursed.

Rakoto's voice brings me back. "My father was a good man. He left to fight the French in '47. He never came back. We never found his body because we did not know where to look. All of the men he was with disappeared too. There was no one to ask. We could not place him in the family crypt or perform the *famadihana.*"

I realize that this woman is not from our island. Her skin is darker than most Malagasy, and her hair is very close to her scalp, different from how Malagasy women often wear their long, straightened hair - braided. She asks my son what the *famadihana* is.

Rakoto laughs lightly and says yes, he is reminded that she is not from here, that things are done very differently in Nairobi. This appears to be a joke between them, because they exchange some banter about how he is from the country, and she is from a large city. I can tell from the way they look at each other that they are in love.

Rakoto tells her that even now, in 1967, with the French no longer in charge and with all the events in the world, such as "Viet Nam," a place that holds no meaning to me, the Malagasy still perform certain rituals. "The *famadihana* is like a party," he explains, "where our dead ancestors are pulled from the family crypt. We take their bodies – just bones, really – and wrap them anew in pristine silk shrouds. The cloth is called *lamba*. We write their names on the *lamba*, and during this process we talk to them. We tell them about what has happened with the family since they died, or since the last *famadihana*, which occurs every seven years or so. And we carry the body around on our shoulders and dance and there is music and it's actually a happy time!" Rakoto bursts into laughter because the look on his mate's face is one of disbelief. "I swear! We consider this essential for the spirit to ascend to Heaven!"

The French no longer in charge. That is what my son said. So Madagascar is finally free from the colonizers! I become dizzy. My concentration fades again. I am both in the room with them and not. I can see the whole of the city, and to me it looks like nothing but ants bustling back and forth. The cars moving through the narrow streets are like leaves the ants carry endlessly between tree and lair. I feel very disconnected from the world, and I feel myself dissolving, becoming less...me. Reality no longer includes me. I am simply an observer and of no consequence to this world at all. But then I recall the wounds I inflicted on the soldier laying with Mikanto. For the briefest time, I smell his blood.

I snap back to attention as Rakoto says my name. He is clinking his glass against hers in a toast, and he has said my name. They are both laughing. She repeats my name and for a moment, I am in the room with them, whole. I feel the bed I am seated on, the soft duvet, the coolness of the air-conditioning. The softness of the carpet tickles the bottoms of my feet. I smell the wine they are toasting my memory with. This happens while they are both tipping their heads back with eyes closed to drink their toast, and then I am ethereal again. I can see and hear, but not feel or smell. Rakoto places his glass on the table, rises and extends his hand to the woman, who takes his with a smile and stands. They kiss and slowly back up until they fall onto the bed, laughing. They begin the process of removing each other's clothes in order to make love. The exhaustion is here again, and I will myself home.

Home. Something I don't have any longer. Where should a *kinoly* reside? Should I be out in the forests, with the lemurs, perched high on a branch, looking down from the canopy? I can no longer haunt a house that doesn't exist.

Instead, I will myself back to my bones. I cannot remember precisely where they are, but at once, I find myself in a shack. It has no door, so I can see the house it belongs to close by. Farming tools hang from nails driven into the ramshackle wood. Yes, this is where I died, on farmland. They have all forgotten that our bones lie beneath their homes and gardens. Or perhaps they never knew.

I sink to my knees and weep tearlessly. I become tired, always the same tiredness stitched to my soul. Outside, the days and nights flicker by.

MORE TIME HAS PASSED when I hear my name spoken. By now, I know it is a simple thing to will myself toward the people using my name. I appear in a small home, at the side of a bed with a small child in it. There are toys scattered on the floor near a toy box. It is dark, a sliver of moonlight peeking through the square window. The boy's mother has just walked out of the room. I think on this and realize that the woman is Mikanto. That would make this child – this boy – my grandchild. The flickering blue of a television in the other room distracts me, so I turn my back to it.

I sit for a long time in silence at the bedside of this child. The sound of the television is low, but I hear snippets of a man reading news. Something about America's bicentennial celebration. Tall ships in New York's harbor. None of these words mean anything to me.

The child turns over and he settles into his pillow more deeply. After a time, his eyes open and go wide at the sight of me. "*Dadabe.*"

Grandfather.

"Do not be afraid, grandson. What is your name?" I ask him, not expecting him to hear me.

"I'm not afraid, *Dadabe*. Momma told me about you. I'm Tsiory. I am eight years old," he adds proudly, with a smile.

"You can hear me?"

"Yes, *Dadabe.*"

"You can see me?" I ask, incredulous.

"Yes, *Dadabe*, because I am asleep. And I'm not afraid, but you do look scary. You have red eyes."

At this, I move a little away from the child. How horrible that he should be visited by a *kinoly*.

"Momma said that you saved her once when she was a little girl. She knows that you don't hurt the family, at least not on purpose."

If I could cry, my tears would flood this entire village. "Tsiory, you are a very brave boy. And a very special boy that you can see me."

"Thank you, *Dadabe*. Momma says you were brave to fight the French. I try to be brave like you were."

The French. I realize that this boy could save me. He could tell them where to look for my body. If only I could tell him where it was.

"I'm tired, *Dadabe*. Momma thinks I'm asleep. But I don't want this dream to end."

"Tsiory, you are a special boy," I repeat. "I am going to leave now and try to find the name of the place where my body lies, so that we can tell your mother."

"Okay, *Dadabe*," he says sweetly, then closes his eyes and turns again to face the wall.

"Tsiory," I say again, wistfully. I remain at his bedside until the blue light of the television goes out. This boy will be my salvation. I could kiss him. I decide to do just that, and cradle his head with one hand and his torso with the other, and plant a phantom kiss on the side of his forehead. The child twitches in his sleep at my touch but is then still.

"Back to your bones," I tell myself.

I reappear in the shed. The sun is rising. I move out of the shed to stand under lightening skies. I have never felt such joy in all these years. I move among the workers, but none of them can see me. I drift toward the main house of the farm. It is a large plantation house with four massive columns dominating the porch. After waiting on the porch for a bit, I lose patience with the closed door and decide to appear in the kitchen. It works. I am standing among the women who wear the same black livery with white highlights. They are bustling about, preparing a midday meal for the workers. None of them see me or otherwise sense me. I sing, I prance, I make a big show of turning in faster and faster circles like a dancer...they have no idea I am there.

I explore the house in search of something that will give me the address, the name of the owner, anything to identify this place. Something I can read and pass along to Tsiory in his dreams. Something he can pass to his mother – my daughter Mikanto – to lead her to my body. I fight off the gathering exhaustion. There is too much work to be done now.

Shortly, I come to a study. It has dark wood décor, with leather chairs and a fireplace. The owners of this farm must be wealthy. I spy a massive desk littered with papers of all types. Finally, I see what I need to see – the masthead from official papers for the farm. *Păturages Paisibles*...the two P's stylized as one large one. I think back to my French lessons...*Peaceful Pastures*. My thoughts darken for a moment at the irony of the name, but then I recall my mission here – to guide Tsiory in setting me free! He will be in school during the day; there is no rush for me to return to him right now.

I will myself to appear in the shed and instantly I am within its dark confines. I repeat the name of the plantation – *Păturages Paisibles* – as a kind of meditation. I feel an emotion that verges on peace.

I am then torn from this state by my name being called – but with such pain and anguish it nearly stuns me. I will myself to the place and find myself back in Tsiory's bedroom.

It is a scene of horror.

Tsiory lies in the same position in which I left him, but his sheets are completely soaked with blood. His blood has dripped from his sheets and pillowcase to the floor and has begun to dry there. His mother – my daughter Mikanto – screams tearfully in the doorway. I cannot tell if she is blocking the path of her other children, or if they are holding her back. She cannot see me; her horror comes from seeing her son. I look down upon poor Tsiory.

There are three deep, bloody holes in his face – on his forehead, near his right eye, and just between his nose and lips. Each corresponds to where I had placed my left hand last night to plant my kiss on him. There are three similar holes in his back where I cradled his body with my right hand. These claws of mine pierced his head and his body. I draw back in horror – and self-loathing – and wither to the opposite end of the room from Mikanto's hysterical crying.

Mikanto again articulates a word in her agonized screaming – my name. She begins chanting it like an angry mantra. I shrink back further into the dark corner of Tsiory's room, praying to any god who will listen to *hide me*. I feel myself become whole, visible. I can smell the death in the room. I feel the hard, dirty floor beneath my feet, the rough bricks pressed against my back. "Fade," I command myself, "fade!"

Mikanto looks sharply in the direction of this corner, confusion flashing across her face. Then she falls forward into the room and lies on the floor. She buries her head in her arms and repeats Tsiory's name. Her other children hover in the doorway; one is a boy of about ten or eleven, and the other is a girl a year or two younger than him. The boy locks eyes with me, but it's impossible to tell if he sees me, or is just averting his gaze from the corpse of his little brother. Neither child cries. The intensity of the boy's gaze threatens to unhinge me from reality forever.

"Monster, back to your bones," I tell myself, and I am gone from the room and back in the shed again. I lie flat on my back and try to drift, to dissolve, to simply stop being—to give in to the tiredness completely. All I have ever brought to my family is death and destruction. It would be better if I were simply in hell. If I were to be tormented by Tsiory's face for the rest of my eternity, it wouldn't be half of what I deserve. Not only am I unworthy of forgiveness for what I have done, but I would refuse if it were offered. I long to trouble this world no more. Days and nights cycle in flashes above my view, and I find a kind of quiet oblivion for a time.

I never cease seeing in this state. There is no way to close my eyes or to dig myself deep underground. I see each day and night that passes, although they mercifully blur into a rhythm that borders on hypnotic. They pass so quickly that men and women retrieving tools from the shed – or any other activities they might partake of in here – are merely flickers of blurs, indecipherable from a leaf blowing in on the winter wind or a lost lemur searching for food.

———

As ALWAYS, someone speaking my name brings me back. The flashing cycle stops immediately, and I stir as if waking, although I have neither rested nor slept.

"Come to me, Grandfather." A young, masculine voice carries to my ear. My name is repeated again. I vow not to touch anything and will myself to the voice.

I appear in the same house – the same room – in which Tsiory died. The walls have been painted a light blue and the furniture has changed; gone is the child's small bed. It looks to be a storage room, but I know that it is the same place. In fact, I have appeared huddled in the same corner, although I did not will myself to do so.

"Grandfather," the young man says with a mixture of awe and confidence. If he fears me, he does not show it.

"I am here, child." I reply, but he does not appear to hear me, he only sees me.

The man sits cross-legged on the floor of the small room. Next to him, there is an earthen bowl with smoke curling up from it. "I am Mendrika. Son of Mikanto and brother to Tsiory."

I am shocked, although it makes no sense for me to be. The young man is at least twenty, maybe even in his mid-twenties. He was the last thing I saw before leaving here so many years ago. After... Tsiory. But this means that another decade has passed in a blink.

Good, I think, *you have spared your family that much of your evil presence, then.*

"I know that you are *kinoly*, Grandfather. And I do not curse you for what you have done. Let your spirit be at ease. I wish to commune and help you."

My anger rises, but not at Mendrika. My self-hatred flares, and I can see from the boy's reaction that my full, true form practically fills the room. From his mind I pull the image of a massive black shape, so tall that its back is bowed against the ceiling. Its eyes are rage red. The arms are held wide, the three claws on each hand are long and lethal. The entire silhouette is framed in a sickly green color. As quickly as it fills the room, the illusion shrinks back down into my wretched form, cowering in the corner. Revulsion courses through me.

Mendrika summons his courage. "Your daughter has died, Grandfather. I wanted you to know that after many years of cursing you for the death of my brother, at the end, she forgave you. It was very difficult for her."

I am stunned and humbled. Mikanto's life was truly cursed by everything I did. For her to have forgiven me means she was a far better person than I ever was.

"I have studied the old ways of our people, Grandfather," he continued, "and I understand – I think I understand – what has happened to you. I know in my heart that you are not evil. I know that you are simply lost."

Lost. For the second time in this room, I could fill the world up with my tears.

"I ask you, as your grandson Mendrika, and in the name of my brother Tsiory, and our mother Mikanto, and her mother Finoana, to guide me to the place where your body lies."

My anger and sadness are now caught up with happiness. I can scarcely contain one emotion at the best of times, but this mixture is dizzying. I try to think of how I can tell the boy where I lie. I find it nearly impossible to focus.

"I know that it is hard for you to know, and it is hard for you to stay for long here."

He is right. Even as he speaks, I grow tired and more distracted.

Mendrika wipes the sweat from his brow with the back of his hand, then hangs his head in exhaustion. "I will summon you again, Grandfather. When I do, bring me information that will set you free."

"Bones." I mutter to myself, tired beyond the telling of it. I appear in the shed and immediately my sight seems to fade, the closest I have been to closing my eyes. I am on the dirt floor of the shed, and I do not fight my exhaustion. I give in to it and my consciousness seems to fade. I am aware, I have sight, but my mind has slowed while the days careen by. I have a vague notion of needing to – somehow – tell Mendrika where I am. I am so very, very tired.

I snap to attention at the sound of my name being called. I recognize the voice as Mendrika's. I do not know how much time has passed. I will myself to him.

"Grandfather, I know that you are with me. I can both see and feel you. Speak and let me hear your voice."

Mendrika's face has filled out since I last beheld him. He is again sitting cross-legged on the floor of the room with a haze of smoke above him. I speak. I yell. Mendrika gives no indication at all that he can hear me. In fact, I see him shake his head and his hands gesture for me to stop.

"I worried this might happen, Grandfather. I can see flashes of you; you appear for a second at a time. But I cannot hear you." He pushes a flat, square box – about the size of his head – across the expanse between us. "I hope this will work for us. In this sand, take your claw and draw for me the place where you lie. Draw a map, or –"

The young man's voice stops as I practically leap across the room to the small box of sand. Despite his earlier bravery, he leans back away from my form. I cannot blame him; the gremlin I can see in his mind is horrible to behold. I think back to how brave Tsiory was to have spoken to me in the dark of night, so close to his bed. *I'm not afraid, but you do look scary. You have red eyes.*

It should be the simplest thing in the world for me to draw the words *"Pâturages Paisibles."* It would take a mortal man mere minutes and no energy at all. Would that I could draw a map from here to there, but I have no sense of where "here" is, especially in relation to the farm. I manage a very large "P" and then find that my strength is sapped. I look to Mendrika with what I hope is a stricken look on my face, and before I know it, I have faded.

The young man looks around the room in confusion and calls my name. While hearing my name sharpens my attention, I cannot manifest a physical form at all. "Bones," I utter. I appear above my grave and attempt to rest again.

Time flies by. I lie with a view of the open shed door. I do my best to count the cycles of day and night. It is difficult, but I land on something close to three hundred and forty days when I hear my name again. Immediately, I will myself to Mendrika.

"Grandfather – our time is short, so I will tell you what I know. You drew a "P" in the sand last year. Your visit to me before that was also a year. It seems this will take time and patience on both of our parts, but I am committed. I will call you to me once a year. Save your energy and simply draw what you can for me, here in the sand."

That means that it has been years since this young man – my grandson – dedicated himself to trying to save me. For me it has seemed like three hours. For him, three years. I marvel briefly, then bend to the task at hand while Mendrika watches. I manage to carve "*ăt*" into the sand before my strength is sapped. Mendrika smiles at me, and I study his round face with awe and love before fading away. "To your bones," I tell myself in relief.

This dance carries on for another fifteen years.

Mendrika's hair is graying lightly at the temples when I finally finish the words. He tells me that he will find this "*Păturages Paisibles*" and that when he calls me again, I should come to him immediately. During the intervening years, I have found a small measure of peace simply by knowing that my grandson is working so hard to help me.

I count exactly three hundred and fifty day and night cycles when my name is spoken again by Mendrika. His voice seems weak. The timbre is off somehow. I fly to him instantly.

"Ah, Grandfather." A racking cough stops the man for a few moments. "Grandfather, I am sick, and I will not last another year."

What passes for my heart sinks with despair. Indeed, the man's hair has thinned and lightened all over, and the wrinkles on his face are deep. He is much older now than I ever lived to be. He sets the box of sand in front of me.

"Please give me more if you can. I have been all over the property you directed me to, but I have not found your body, and the owners of the farm are losing patience with me. We are using metal detectors in hope of finding any bullet casings, and a friend of mine in the Antananarivo police has loaned us a cadaver dog twice. But we haven't found anything yet." A cough racks his body. "I have enlisted my wife and my oldest son to help in case I..." Mendrika can't continue. "This is Regina, my wife, and our son... Tsiory." He gestures to the regal woman standing behind him, and the young man next to her. The boy – who is nearly a fully grown man – is lean but muscular, and has piercing, dark eyes, like his grandmother...my daughter Mikanto.

Until I heard his son's name, I had been bent to the task of drawing the word "shed" in the sand. I look up at them, my energy draining with each passing second. They named their son Tsiory – what an honor the boy carries. Regina covers her mouth in fear at the sight of me, a wrinkled gremlin hunched over a small box of sand, but Tsiory steps around his father and guesses at the word I am making.

"She," Tsiory says. "Shell, shelf. Sheep. Father, were there sheep on that farm?"

Mendrika beams with pride. "No, my son. It's a mango and passion-fruit plantation."

Tsiory's face wrinkles in concentration. "Sheet. Sheer. Shears." He lifts his head, an idea blooming. "Shed?"

I nearly reach for the boy, but immediately think better of it, given the daggers on the ends of my hands. Instead, I channel everything within me to hit the box of sand. I send it across the floor, upsetting it so much that the box lands upside down. Sand litters the room. Regina startles and turns from the room to walk briskly away.

Mendrika and Tsiory are in awe. They look at each other with cautious joy. "Shed?" they say in unison.

I feel myself fading, but I fight to stay. The men have moved their attention from the box and from the ghost in the room and are quizzing each other about the presence of a shed on the farm. I am not able to stay long enough to hear what they decide. Against my will, I find myself again in the shed, tired to the point of complete shutdown.

Thirty days and nights pass.

I am still in the shed when I hear a familiar voice. I recognize it as Tsiory's. Soon, his frame fills the open doorway. He is flanked by two older men, both rough-looking and sweaty.

"Nobody likes to go here," one says. "It's always cold."

"I tried to bring a girl here once. She said the hairs on the back of her neck were standing up. I kissed her there but she told me to take her someplace different or it was off," the other says.

I see Tsiory smile. "Is this it, grandfather?" he mutters under his breath.

I gather all my strength and reach for one of the tools – a pair of pruning shears – and cause them to fall blade first into the soil of the shed floor.

Tsiory's mouth drops open in shock, but then his smile returns almost immediately. The two men with him peer over his shoulder, asking variations on the question "what happened?" Tsiory turns and smoothly guides both men away. Their voices fade.

I am hopeful for Tsiory's return, but I begin to despair as the days and nights start streaming by again. The shears remain embedded in the dirt, forming an X.

FOUR HUNDRED AND forty-seven days pass. I have fallen into anguish when my attention is seized by the image of Tsiory standing in the door-frame again. He has said my name. He looks sad as he hunkers down on his haunches to address me. He looks at the wrong wall, but how is he supposed to know where I perch?

"Grandfather, my father died last week. The cancer finally caught up with him and he is gone." Tsiory pauses, wipes tears from his cheeks, dabs at his nose with a handkerchief. "But I have not forgotten about you." The young man collects himself and stands. "I have been in negotiations with the owners of this place to dig here. They are penny-pinching bastards, I assure you. They are insisting that we build a brand-new shed for them once this one is demolished for the dig. I have also checked at the library in Antananarivo, and one of the historians there said there are some vague records of a group of rebels disappearing in this general area. I think it's just a matter of time – and money – before we're able to excavate here."

Tsiory picks the pruning shears out of the dirt, having to tug on them a bit harder than he expected. He bangs them once against the outside of his boot, then selects a nail to hang them from. After this, he turns to go, but then turns back and speaks quietly into the darkness of the shed. "I don't expect you'll see him, since we have his body in the family crypt in Anjiro. But Grandfather, if you see my father's spirit, please tell him how much I love him. And that I miss him."

He is gone, and I remain in the shed. I am at relative peace, but anger with the property owners licks at my mind. I will myself to the main house of the sprawling plantation and move slowly to the porch. I am about to put myself inside, but I recall that Tsiory has just left. If I were to cause mischief so soon after his visit, they might suspect Tsiory of pulling some sort of hoax. I decide to wait. I try to reason out a way to force the owner's hand to make this easier for Tsiory.

I sit invisible on the porch. People going in and out of the house hurry by, unsure of why they feel so unsettled near me. I wonder how many times in my life I stood in the presence of spirits and did not know it... passed it off as a chill or a strange feeling. I have been a ghost for nearly fifty years, twice as long as I was ever a man. My patience evaporates at this thought, and I will myself into the house, directly to the study.

There is a portly, frowning white man sitting at the desk. He gazes deeply into a large, tan television sitting on a corner of the desk. There is a rectangle with buttons on it in front of him, and his right hand rests on a small, oblong object connected to a thin cord which runs behind the television. He presses buttons on the rectangle with a confused look on his face, shifting his concentration between the screen and the rectangle. He pauses only long enough to lathe sweat away from his forehead with a meaty index finger. This man would not notice me even if I were visible.

I move through the house, willing myself to pass through walls. I can do this with ease. If only I had known such skills earlier. If only I had known what my touch would do. No one taught me to be what I am. There was no guide, no set of rules. If I could see other spirits and teach them, I would. I move to the first floor again.

I pass through a communal dining room, where at least twenty of the workers sit and wolf down their afternoon meals. Sweat drips onto their plates. Most of them scowl when not chewing. There is no conversation, no sense of camaraderie among them. I move back to the second floor of the house.

I come upon a bedroom. Two people are having sex on top of the made bed. They are continually *shushing* each other in an attempt at silence. They appear oblivious to the squeaks emanating from the coiling and uncoiling mattress springs. I see a pile of clothes on the floor that seem to belong to one of the workers – the man's. I recognize the woman as one who worked in the kitchen years ago. Her black dress is hiked up over her pudgy midsection and her arms are raised above her head in ecstasy. The man slows his thrusts as I pass through them. The woman opens her eyes and looks around the room in confusion. They are both distracted by my presence despite not being able to see me. There is a wedding ring on her finger, but none on his. I keep moving, and their furtive movements resume.

I pass through more bedrooms, empty as they should be at this hour. Bathrooms both occupied and not. One man slumbers while sitting upon a bucket in a broom closet, his elbow on his knee and his head against his fist. Some residents of the house appear to sense my passing, while others are completely oblivious. I end up back down in the bustling kitchen. At least two of the women wear annoyance on their faces, no doubt due to the absence of their fornicating friend.

I decide to return to my shed. There is nothing I could do to these people that they are not already doing to themselves in some way or another; nothing that would make them acquiesce to Tsiory's requests any more quickly than they are going to anyway. I am very tired again. I know that I can put my trust in my great-grandson; Tsiory will deliver me. I have waited this long. I can wait a while longer.

K'CETNOC & THE
ETERNAL JOURNEY,
PART 1: KEVIN

B rittani's phone dings, indicating the arrival of a text message. She turns her head slowly on the pillow, eyes still closed against the early morning sun fighting its way past the pastel drapes. Another ding, and her eyes open. One more ding, and she slaps her arms against the bed in frustration, groans, and reaches for the phone on the nightstand, upsetting the small dog sleeping at her still-covered feet. She groans.

Sitting against the Western wall of her bedroom, pointedly soaking up the sunlight, the lapidarian earthly avatar of K'cetnoc, Keeper of Planets and Warden of Sol, perks up. After a minute of quiet in which the *bloop* of Brittani scrolling through multiple texts is the only sound, K'cetnoc asks, "WHO IS IT?"

"Just Cyndi. But there are a buttload of texts from Kevin I don't even remember *seeing* last night."

"BRITTANI WAS INEBRIATED MOST OF LAST EVENING." K'cetnoc's tone is gravelly.

"Ugh, tell me about it. I got fuckin' *way-sted*."

"IT WAS NEARLY AS BAD AS THE NIGHT K'CENTOC AND BRITTANI MET, WHEN BRITTANI INDICATED THAT BRITTANI HAD 'MIXED MUSHROOMS, EXTRA LOUD EDIBLES, AND THEN FELL DOWN A MASSIVE FECKING K-HOLE.'"

"Feels like it, yeah," Brittani murmurs.

"REMIND K'CETNOC WHICH ONE KEVIN IS, AGAIN."

"He's that one douche I hooked up with about a month ago."

Beebee, the Pomeranian mix, jumps down from the bed and settles next to the mineral-studded bulk of K'cetnoc's left leg and resumes sleeping.

"THE ONE WITH THE OVERSIZED APPENDAGE?"

"Yeah, 'Tripod,' that's him."

"WHAT DOES THE ONE CALLED 'CYNDI' WANT?"

Brittani quotes the text message: "'**Betch, getcho ass outta bed for brunch!**'"

"BRITTANI DOES NOT LOOK LIKE BRITTANI WANTS TO CONSUME SUSTENANCE," K'cetnoc observes, absently stroking Beebee's back with a lithic finger.

"Oh my god, no, but I would fucking kill for a Bloody Mary right now."

"GOOD. BRITTANI SHOULD STAY IN BED. K'CETNOC WILL KEEP BRITTANI COMPANY."

Brittani is frowning at her phone, which is now dinging with true purpose. Her thumbs are nearly a blur of motion as she replies.

"K'CETNOC AND BRITTANI COULD CUDDLE AGAIN, LIKE LAST-"

Brittani launches herself from bed with a sound of exasperation that continues all the way into her small bathroom. The wall which the massive, rocky being leans against divides it from the bedroom proper. K'cetnoc and Beebee watch her progress.

"K'CETNOC APOLOGIZES FOR—"

"Huh? Oh, no, honey – it's Cyndi. She only wants me there because there's this bartender that she's trying to hook up with. But she doesn't wanna look desperate and wants me to meet his friend who works there, too. As if I would date a *waiter*! But she's being super extra."

"K'CETNOC UNDERSTANDS. K'CETNOC IS WILLING TO WAGER THAT THIS 'WAITER' IS NOT GOOD ENOUGH FOR BRITTANI. CYNDI SHOULD CONSIDER REMAINING IN CYNDI'S ALLOCATED PORTION OF THE THOROUGHFARE."

"She should *stay in her lane*, 'Cet, but yes...you are so right." Brittani corrects the ancient, cosmic being and continues applying her mascara.

K'cetnoc stands gently, doing his best not to upset the dog, who is once again asleep. He rounds the small corner so he can speak to Brittani face to face, or face to mirror, such as it is. Brittani is wearing nothing but a lacy, see-through bra and thong underwear. K'cetnoc makes an unintelligible sound of apology and surprise.

Brittani stops stroking her eyelashes and fixes him with a reflected coy smile. "Oh, it's fine, 'Cet. We're buddies. I don't care if you see me like this."

K'cetnoc knows the answer to the query before he asks but chooses to anyway. "WHAT IS 'BUD-DEES'?"

Brittani resumes doing her makeup, then pauses briefly to adjust each breast, one at a time, accentuating their positions in her low-cut bra. "Friends, you know. I can tell you anything! Companions."

"COMPANIONS." K'cetnoc repeats. "IT IS GOOD TO HAVE BRITTANI DiMARCO AS A COMPANION. K'CETNOC HAS BEEN IN EXISTENCE SINCE THE SUN GATHERED ELEMENTS AND IGNITED. K'CETNOC WATCHED AS THE DUST SPUN

AND SLOWLY COALESCED INTO PLANETOIDS. K'CETNOC BORE WITNESS TO THE COLLISION BETWEEN BRITTANI'S WORLD AND ANOTHER, WHICH, IN TIME, FORMED THE MOON-"

"Son of a *bitch*!" Brittani curses, her attention on her phone again. K'cetnoc hears the mascara pen hit the bathroom counter. A flurry of clicks ensues, indicating another torrent of texts being sent. Disturbed by his owner's voice, Beebee lifts his head toward the bathroom.

"CYNDI?" K'cetnoc struggles to keep the disappointment out of his voice.

Brittani continues texting furiously. K'cetnoc thinks that perhaps she did not hear or is ignoring him. "No, no," she answers, her voice tinged with frustration and impatience, "now it's Kevin. He's trying to guilt-trip me into hooking up with him again later today."

"KEVIN, WHO IS A DOUCHE," K'cetnoc observes.

"Yeah," Brittani is again distracted, but also paying close attention to the lipstick she is applying. "He wants me to go hiking with him later. And I really want to, because I've been trying to figure out when I could hit Los Liones."

"HIKING IS BENEFICIAL TO BRITTANI'S CARDIOVAS-CULAR SYSTEM."

"Yeah. But I know he just wants to get me alone."

"THEN BRITTANI SHOULD NOT GO."

"Yeah. But I want to, kinda."

"K'CETNOC DOES NOT TRUST THIS 'KEVIN' BEING."

"Yeah. I'll be lucky to get out of this with just a bee-jay," Brittani mutters to her reflection.

"K'CETNOC DID NOT HEAR BRITTANI JUST NOW."

"Mmm, nothing." Brittani is primping her hair, her shiny, maroon fingernails peeking out thrust after thrust through her chestnut mane.

Brittani turns from the mirror finally and moves out of the bathroom, past K'cetnoc and Beebee, who raises his head to track her progress. Brittani opens her wardrobe and stands momentarily with her left fist on her hip.

"IT IS CURRENTLY TWENTY DEGREES CELSIUS OUTSIDE.

IT WILL WARM UP TO TWENTY-FIVE OR –SIX LATER. BRIT-
TANI SHOULD DRESS IN LAYERS," K'cetnoc offers helpfully.

"It's what now?" Brittani has selected a pair of black, spandex yoga
pants and is pulling them on over her thighs.

"SIXTY-EIGHT FARENHEIT, RISING TO SEVENTY-EIGHT
LATER." K'cetnoc looks at Beebee, who rolls his eyes and places his snout
between his paws.

Brittani moves each hanging top aside with a flick of her left hand,
attempting to settle on a look which will serve her well both for brunch
and a hike later on.

"THE MAROON KAREN SCOTT V-NECK WILL WORK
NICELY FOR BOTH ACTIVITIES."

Brittani selects the suggested top from the wardrobe and holds it up
against her torso. "Yeah, thanks 'Cet, that works!"

"BRITTANI IS WELCOME; HOWEVER, K'CETNOC STILL
FEELS THAT BRITTANI SHOULD NOT—"

Brittani's attention is back on the phone. "Oh my god, girl...I'm
coming!" she both vocalizes and texts, frowning.

"K'CETNOC WILL BE HERE UPON BRITTANI'S RETURN,"
K'cetnoc states ruefully as Brittani rushes back and forth in front of him,
searching for her purse.

Brittani calls from the hallway, moments away from disappearing
through her front door, "Thanks 'Cet. Can you please take Beebee out in
a bit? Please please please? Byeeeeee!"

The door shuts with a *thunk* and K'cetnoc and Beebee are left alone,
gazing at each other.

"Don't look at me, dude. I think you're a total catch." Beebee barks
gently.

"THANK YOU, BEEBEE. BEEBEE IS A GOOD BOY."

"Oh, I know." Beebee stands and stretches all four legs, arching his
tiny back. "And Kevin is a total dick. She'll probably end up dating him
for, like, four months." With that, the dog leaps back onto Brittani's
unmade bed, curls into a small circle, and falls asleep.

"GODDAMMIT," K'cetnoc says to no one in particular.

BURYING ATTILA

O*h shit*, Aoric thought. *Who died now?*
Aoric knew from the hooting and hollering of the horde that *something* important had happened. Three horsemen thundered by the open doorway of the small hut he shared with two dozen other slaves. Aoric backed into the hut to avoid being splattered with churned dirt and manure. Each of the horsemen's cheeks had been rent by small cuts, the blood streaming horizontally to their ears in their haste. An orange glow to the south indicated a colossal bonfire; he could smell the smoke drifting into the encampment now.

Turning from the street, Aoric looked over the faces of the men in the hut. The slaves ranged from young to old, the colors of their skin touching every hue known to man – if you could see past the layers of dirt. Each man looked toward Aoric with eyebrows raised, a question dangling on every tongue, none of which had tasted enough wine tonight to deal with whatever the answer was.

Aoric shrugged noncommittally and returned to his bunk, then slumped against the wall which served as his headboard.

"Useless *Goth*," one man spat, rising to stalk toward the open doorway with long strides.

This one – one of the *Alans*, as the Romans called them – was a recent arrival into the Hun's servitude. Aoric knew him only as a tall, young, blonde malcontent who spoke without hesitating to think. That the Alan had referred to him as "Goth" rather than his true nationality – *Grethungi* – told Aoric all he needed to know about how the Alan had come to be in the service of the mighty Attila's Horde.

The Romans were the ones assigning new names to everything. *Grethungi* were Goths. *Massagetae* were Alans. And the Huns? Well, they were simply *Barbarians*. That meant the Alan had been sold by the Romans to Attila's Horde, or possibly liberated from Roman slavery to be annexed into Hunnish slavery. Either way, it didn't matter to Aoric. Brash, angry, young men arrived weekly and disappeared just as frequently. Their faces were a blur. Aoric ignored the man's insult, folded his hands across his chest, and closed his eyes in a posture of relaxation.

In a far corner of the hut, a man shitting into a chamber pot farted wetly.

The Alan, his hands posted on either side of the door jamb, was issuing reports with abrupt vagueness. "Three more riders. Big bonfire over there."

"Where?" one of the slaves asked with annoyance.

Aoric's eyes were still closed, so he wasn't sure which man had spoken. This was exactly why he hadn't told his compatriots anything...because he didn't know anything. *Why report the news without the pertinent facts? Why give bits and pieces? All will be revealed in time.*

"Where what?" the Alan barked to the annoyed slave.

"Where is the bonfire?" the slave replied.

All the Alan did in response was tip his head in the direction of the fire —in this case, south. Aoric wondered if it was possible the man didn't know his north from his south.

"To the right?" the exasperated slave asked.

Aoric waited a beat, and then said in a loud, clear voice, "South. To the south, about a mile." His eyes were still closed, but by the way the scent on the air changed, Aoric could tell that everyone's head had swiveled in his direction.

Ignoring the undermining tone of Aoric's announcement, the Alan proclaimed, "Many of these riders are bleeding from their mouths."

"Is the encampment under attack?" asked a different slave, this one allowing panic into his voice. Aoric heard his sandals hit the dirt floor as the slave's anxiety drove him to his feet.

Aoric did not want to wait for the Alan's opinion on this query, so he opened his eyes, uncrossed his arms, and wearily swung his own feet off the bed to the floor. "Huns rend their own flesh when they mourn. They cut their hair, tear their clothes, and cut their cheeks."

The Alan had turned to look at Aoric along with every other man in the hut. He scowled at Aoric but said nothing to contradict him. Horses galloping by churned up dirt and shit that landed on the Alan's shins and knees.

"So, who died?" someone in the back of the hut called out, possibly the man on the chamber pot.

Aoric merely shrugged again.

"I bet it was Onegesius," the Alan speculated, now turned to face the men in the hut. He ignored the filth on his legs. "Or another one of Attila's lieutenants."

"I hope it was that old bat Priscus," someone offered.

"That miserable Roman bastard," another slave chimed in.

"Hey, easy now...I'm Roman," yet another man called.

The hut descended into cacophony. Threats were made, and oaths sworn.

By now, Aoric had drifted closer to the door, and, unfortunately, the smelly Alan. His attention was on the tension brewing among his brethren, and so he did not see the three hulking Hun warriors come to the door of the hut behind him.

The rabble went silent and wide-eyed. Aoric said loudly into the sudden silence, "Maybe it's Attila himself who has died."

The Alan backhanded Aoric on the left shoulder. Aoric whirled to retaliate but then saw the Huns ducking their heads to enter the hut.

One of them narrowed his eyes at Aoric and the Alan in turn.

"What do you know?" he growled.

The Alan looked to Aoric, his eyebrows raised as if to say *Yes, Mister Know-It-All Goth, what* do *you know?*

"Good evening to you," Aoric offered.

In return, the warrior grabbed Aoric by the back of the neck and pulled him out into the street. The Alan started complaining, so Aoric knew he had been secured as well.

Away from the rest of the men in the hut, the Hun warriors leaned menacingly close to Aoric and repeated, "*What* do you know?"

Aoric stammered a bit, looking at the massive shoulders and biceps of each Hun warrior in turn. "I, uh, know that your customs...when someone important dies..."

After a long pause, the Huns raised their eyebrows in expectation.

"That there is much commotion, and...the rending of flesh, and clothes, and uh, hair. And that a fire is made. The greater the fire, the greater the, uh, leader."

"This is true, Goth," a new voice uttered in crisp, clipped tones to Aoric's left.

Aoric turned and beheld an older man, clearly neither a warrior nor a Hun, clothed in a toga that used to be white but was now soiled with dirt and age. His gray hair was clipped in the Roman fashion, and he had an air of nobility.

Behind them, the Alan muttered, "Oh, fuck."

SHORTLY THEREAFTER, Aoric and the sullen Alan found themselves next to a moist riverbed.

Suffocating fish flopped, water plants reeked of decay. The river had been dammed about a mile upstream, and several Hun warriors worked to set up another, smaller dam about thirty meters downstream. This smaller dam would ensure that no water would find its way back to where the men were to do their work.

According to the elder Roman Priscus, who stood out of reach of the smell of the drying riverbed, Aoric and the Alan were to dig a grave for none other than the ruler of the steppes, Attila the Hun. Every time Priscus said the leader's name, the nearby Hunnish warriors standing guard would bark wounded cries into the night air. After a few instances of this, Priscus simply referred to Attila as "the departed."

"Yours is a truly heroic sacrifice," Priscus concluded without further elaboration.

Aoric and the Alan looked at each other, their hands still bound with rope, and mouthed "'Sacrifice?'"

When they turned back to where the Roman had been standing, they found instead a single Hun warrior on horseback. His bow was slung over his shoulder, and he held a three-meter-long spear in his left hand. In his right were two torches.

Once Priscus and his retinue had ridden away, the guard urged his horse forward a few steps. "You." The guard thrust his chin out in Aoric and the Alan's direction. "Come take this torch."

The men looked at each other again and shrugged. After an awkward minute, the Alan sighed loudly, marched to the guard, and took the proffered torch.

"The shovels will come later. Start digging." He thrust his chin out again, this time in the vague direction of the muck that comprised the riverbed.

While the Alan trudged toward the embankment, Aoric cleared his throat and offered his tied hands up to the guard.

"What?"

"Do you think we could have our hands unbound?"

"No."

"Why not?"

The guard raised an eyebrow. "*Why not?*"

"Yes, why not?"

The guard let out an exasperated sigh. "Look, you're going to be scooping up wet mud with both hands and tossing it to the side. Your hands are going to be next to each other anyway. What does it matter if they're bound?"

"It's uncomfortable."

"Friend, that is not my problem."

"We're friends now?"

"Fine. Slave. Goth. Whatever you wish. Your comfort is not my concern."

"What if we need water? Or food?" Aoric persisted. By now, the Alan had stopped his descent and turned to see if Aoric's tactics would work or if the man would be speared where he stood.

54

"I have a skin with some water. Food will arrive later. *After* you do some actual work."

"Alright. This just seems a little uncivilized." Aoric turned on his heel and headed toward the Alan, who did the same and continued down to the riverbank.

The Hun shook his head for a few moments as the two ambled away. "Is this your first day in slavery or something?" he muttered in their direction.

AORIC MOVED AS FAR AWAY AS possible from the Alan, who seemed to never tire of talking. A few hours had passed since they'd started tossing mud out of the riverbank, and Aoric's arms were screaming with ache. How the Alan had enough energy to natter on *and* toss handful after disgusting handful of muck over his shoulder, Aoric would never know.

"Once I am out of here, I will escape from these idiots." The Alan hazarded a look at the distant Hun guard, who glowered at them from his horse about ten meters away. "Then it is a simple matter of finding the gap between the Carpates Mountains and the Sarmatian Mountains, keep heading northeast, and then home."

Aoric stopped digging, looked at the Alan for a long moment, and then yawned.

"You will see, Goth. You are too old for the trip, or I would take you with me. But you would never make it."

This remark eroded the last of Aoric's good nature. He stood, shook his hands and arms loose of clinging mud, and started making his way toward the Alan. Both of them had lost their sandals early in the proceedings, so it required some effort to pull each foot out of the muck.

The Alan stopped his own work and watched Aoric approach, only rising to his full height when Aoric was a meter away.

"Look, you pompous ass," Aoric said into the Alan's chest, then raised his head to look the man in the eye.

To his credit, the Alan wore a look of bemusement rather than spoiling for a fight.

"We're never getting out of this riverbed alive," Aoric continued. "You *do* know that, right?"

The Alan's face slackened a bit, his smile dropping away. He looked over his left shoulder at the mounted Hun. The guard was yawning, his mouth pointed to the sky as if screeching a victory cry. The Alan returned his gaze to Aoric. "Why do you think this, Goth?"

"*Goth*," Aoric said caustically. "My name is Aoric, Alan. What is yours?"

Rather than answer him, the Alan repeated his question. "Why do you think this, Aoric the Goth?"

Aoric shook his head, looking briefly at his feet, which had sunk about six inches into the muck. "You would never be able to escape them. There are patrols from here to the eastern mountains. They are on horseback and will run you down with ease."

The Alan merely shrugged his huge shoulders.

"But more importantly, they are never going to let us out of this river-bank, as I said. Why do you think they chose the two of us rather than the entire team of slaves?"

The Alan's mouth curled and his brow furrowed, which indicated to Aoric that he was in deep thought. Aoric hoped the Alan didn't hurt himself in the process.

Aoric continued without waiting. "The last of Attila's lieutenants to die was given a massive funeral. He was buried with five slaves, two of his wives, a chest full of Roman gold and another chest full of his wives' jewelry."

The Alan's face scrunched up, and he raised his right eyebrow. "So?"

"So, the slaves that dug that grave never returned."

The Alan looked suspicious. "Perhaps they were freed for their efforts. And if they did not return, how do you have this information about what the man was buried with?"

"Because when I saw the funeral procession pass by our hut, his two dead wives were in a cart followed by five slaves. Four of them were carrying the chests, each holding a side. The fifth one, bringing up the rear, was just outright weeping."

"That is a huge international leap," the Alan said smugly.

"*Inferential*, you moron. And no, it is not. Think about it. If anyone knew where that grave was, what would be the first thing they would do?"

"Leave flowers?"

Aoric began to speak, but the Alan held up his hands.

"I am joking. Your point is made, Goth...Aoric. If anyone knew where that grave was, they would rob it. Of course."

Aoric's face relaxed a bit. Maybe the Alan wasn't quite as dim as he appeared to be. "So, if it's truly Attila that has died – and I suspect it *is* due to their reaction at our hut – then how much treasure would *he* be buried with?"

The Alan's face went slack, then white. "Pretty much all of it."

"Exactly. We have as long to live as it takes us to dig this grave."

"So we have until then to figure out how to get out of this mess." The Alan's eyes looked left, then right.

"You're kidding, right? There *is* no way out of this mess, Alan. We are doomed."

The Alan scoffed. "Speak for yourself, old man. I will not go down without a fight."

They were interrupted by the Hun guard calling to them, but they were unable to hear his words. Both slaves turned and held their hands up in confusion. The guard urged his mount forward, slowly. The men watched the guard's horse skirt the soft edge of riverbank cautiously. Both hoped he would tip over. It was their only chance.

The guard stopped, cupped his hands over his mouth, then yelled, "Stop talking and get back to work!"

The Alan took the opportunity to try his luck. "Say, brother, what time do we get to stop and head back to camp?"

The Hun wrinkled his nose in disgust. "You are not my brother, Alan. And neither of you get to stop, or to head back to camp."

The Alan looked at Aoric, who wore a knowing look on his face.

"We can't work without sleep. Or food and drink, for that matter," the Alan called.

"You can sleep on the riverbank, right where I am. Under my spear and bow. But not yet. Now get back to work!"

"Or what?" The Alan posted his hands on his hips, defiantly.

The guard, who had ridden over with his bow in his hands in addition to the reins of the horse, reached over his shoulder, nocked an arrow, and sent it flying through the flesh at the top of the Alan's left ear. Aoric and the Alan didn't have time to react before the arrow was lodged in the riverbank sludge.

"Ow," the Alan muttered, then both he and Aoric again bent to the task of flinging muck out of the riverbed.

———

SOME TIME LATER, after the sun had risen and started burning their shoulders, the Hun guard called them over to the edge of the riverbank. On it was a full skin of water, and the men proceeded to wash the mud from their arms and legs. Their Hun guard was now nowhere to be seen, but they found themselves too fatigued to consider escaping. They both lay on their backs in the grass, content for the moment to be out of the reeking mire they'd spent the last twelve-plus hours flinging.

The Alan detected it first: a scent of meat and of bread, and possibly wine. Both men rose and scaled the rest of the slope of the riverbank. There, they found several Hun guards mounted on horseback, a hulking Hun general, and the diminutive Roman, Priscus. All these men were standing near a wooden table holding the feast the men had smelled. Aoric and the Alan's stomachs overcame any sense of umbrage they held at the task forced on them, and the still-manacled men stumbled forward.

Priscus seated himself on a stool, his hand cradling a pewter cup of wine, and gestured to the slaves with his free hand. "Come, gentlemen. Eat. You must be famished."

Neither man acknowledged him; they simply started tearing apart the offered food. Aoric started with a light course of fruits and bread while the Alan ripped both drumsticks from one of the cooked fowl on the table, then devoured each successively.

The Hun general snorted. At least, Aoric thought it was the general and not one of the horses nearby. Aoric hazarded a look at the man, squinting to do so in the gleaming sunlight.

Priscus spoke up. "This is Onegesius, one of Attila's most trusted lieutenants." He was interrupted briefly by the Huns howling a brief cry into the morning air. With a wince, Priscus continued. "He and his men are fasting as part of the mourning for...the departed. Onegesius does not see the point in feeding men condemned to a fate such as yours, but, well..." He trailed off.

"But he knows enough to feed his workforce if he wants the job done, eh?" Aoric said around a mouthful of bread, finishing Priscus' point but looking pointedly at Onegesius.

"Oh, that the sun would not bother to rise on such a terrible day!" Onegesius said, loud enough for the Hun contingent to hear, refusing to look at Aoric or the Alan. "All is lost, and all of the tasks of men are folly." He bowed his head and stared deeply into the grass at his feet.

"Uh-huh," Aoric said. "Well, good Priscus, we appreciate your efforts. Do you think there's any chance we could be rid of these bindings?" He raised his hands slightly, his grip threatening to drop the greasy meat he was now holding.

"Oh, my dear Goth, that is not up to me. And what *is* the point of freedom, after all? I was sent here by Rome, free to document Hunnish rule and custom. But now my mission is cut short with the..." Priscus glanced around guiltily. "The extinguishment of the glorious sun itself!"

"The sun has gone out!" Onegesius flailed his massive arms dramatically and wandered away from the table. Two of the mounted Huns turned their horses to follow, then thought better of it and simply watched him go.

Priscus switched to a more conspiratorial tone and continued complaining into his wine. "Honestly, I was making real inroads with these barbari – with these noble warriors. Theodosius isn't going to hold that senate seat forever." He looked up at the men as if to say *but you know how that goes, right?*

The Alan was oblivious and had changed his tactics, taking huge hunks of bread and sticking the dripping poultry between them, then biting chunks out of the entire concoction. Aoric looked at Priscus unwaveringly and then nodded. He realized there was no point in interrupting a Roman agonizing about his ambitions.

Priscus muttered something inaudible and drained his cup with a frown. After a moment spent staring into the dregs, he set the cup down, slapped his hands on his thighs, and rose from the stool. "Well, gentlemen, I wish you the best, but it's time to return to the river. That grave won't dig itself." The look on his face told Aoric that the Roman thought he was actually imparting great knowledge.

In response, the Alan started stuffing his cheeks full like a drunken chipmunk. Aoric waited for Priscus to turn and wander toward the mounted Huns, then rammed as much bread into his tunic as he could manage in the few seconds he had.

One of the Huns rode forward, then tossed two roughly hewn shovels to the ground near the slaves. The guard stared pointedly at them until they disengaged from the table. After wiping their greasy hands on the grass, the slaves picked up the shovels by their wooden handles and started back down to the river. Aoric hazarded one last look over his shoulder and saw Priscus walking next to Onegesius, who himself was nearly doubled over with grief. All but one of the mounted Hun retinue followed in their wake.

The Alan and Aoric were alone again, save for their single mounted Hunnish guard and the forgotten water skin. They ambled back into the muck and resumed digging.

In relatively short order, the men were able to make real progress with the shovels. They were now out of their guard's sight by virtue of having dug a hole deeper than the Alan's height, which Aoric estimated as six and a half feet. Aoric, himself nearly a foot shorter, wouldn't be able to extricate himself from the hole without help; a fact that played heavily into his sour mood.

"Why are you so down, Goth? Er, Aoric?" the Alan asked pointedly.

Aoric looked at the top of the hole, then at his lower body, then back at the Alan.

The Alan stood with a blank look on his face, leaning on the handle of his shovel.

"I'm never getting out of this hole alive, Alan." Aoric had resumed digging, and the Alan barely heard his muttered reply.

The Alan went back to digging as well, his back to Aoric. "Not with that attitude, no."

Aoric turned and spat. "Not with any attitude, Alan. It is time for you to face reality. You and I will be dead before the next dawn."

The Alan turned to meet Aoric's gaze. He shook his head gently and graced Aoric with a smile. "By the next dawn, I will be mostly to the mountains. By the dawn after that, I will be back in my wife's arms. I will sleep with her for days, our daughter cradled between us. I will scarcely leave my house for a week."

Aoric opened his mouth to reply, then simply turned again and jabbed his shovel into the dense clay of the grave.

"I know you do not agree with me, Goth. You will see. The last you shall see of me will be my back. Let them bring a hundred Huns on their vaunted horses to chase me; they will never catch me. I will be the very shadows."

Aoric turned and uttered an exhausted sigh. "Alan?"

"Goth?"

"If you are truly so talented at evading Huns, how were you caught in the first place?"

The Alan stammered for a moment, then his face darkened. "You don't know my people, Goth Aoric."

"Just 'Aoric.'" Aoric sighed again.

The Alan ignored him. "If one of my people dies hiding, then he is always hiding. If one of them dies free, in his own bed, in his own house, then that is where he always is – free."

Aoric's brow wrinkled in thought. He was starting to see the Alan's point.

"If I die in this..." The Alan looked as though he might lose his composure for a second, but his voice strengthened again almost immediately. "If I were to die in this *hole*, Aoric, then I would *always* be in this hole."

Aoric nodded lightly. "If you were to die trying to escape, which means you are free, then you are always free."

The Alan nodded, wearing a wan smile that didn't quite wrinkle his eyes. "Always free," he repeated.

Aoric conceded the argument with a genuine smile and waited for the Alan to turn from him and resume work.

Instead, the Alan leaned again on the handle of his shovel. His voice lowered to a conspiratorial level. "And if you wish, Aoric, I will boost you out of this pit before I escape."

Unspoken was the understanding that the Alan would not wait for Aoric. He would not be burdened with anyone's fate but his own.

Aoric nodded grimly and turned from his companion to continue digging. One thing the Alan said kept repeating in his mind as he dug.

I would always be in this hole...

A plan began taking shape in Aoric's mind.

———

OVER THE INTERVENING HOURS, Aoric had laid out the plan to the Alan as they worked. The tall man had remained mostly silent, but offered no rebuttal to any individual aspect, which Aoric took as tacit agreement. The time to act was now, however, as the slightest hint of light showed in the Eastern sky. Escape during midday would be a brutally short escapade.

The two men faced each other, saying nothing. The Alan extended his right arm, and Aoric grasped his forearm. They locked eyes, then released each other's forearms and leaned their shovels against the wall of the tomb. The Alan severed his perfectly, using his foot to break the shovel where the shaft met the metal of the shovelhead. After a few tries, Aoric was able to break his as well, although a little more of the wooden shaft stayed with the head of his shovel.

As planned, the Alan clambered out of the pit cautiously to avoid catching the eye of their Hunnish guard. As soon as the big man was safely out, lying in the mud on the edge of it, Aoric tossed the shovelheads up to the Alan one at a time. The long wooden shafts would remain with Aoric in the tomb. The Alan disappeared from view.

Aoric turned to the eastern wall of the tomb and pulled a few loose pieces of clay down from the imprint that was carved there, an Aoric-sized indentation that he would press himself into and then cover with mud and clay. Already there lay a large mass of both to his left. All that remained was for the Alan to return with several of a crucial item.

Mere moments had passed before the Alan returned, signaling his presence by dropping one of the riverbank reeds into the tomb. Aoric caught the last couple before they hit the mud of the tomb floor, then nodded a final farewell to the Alan. True to his word, the last thing Aoric saw of the Alan was his filthy, naked back.

Aoric worked fast, securing several shortened lengths of the reeds in his tunic, next to the bread that he hoped would sustain him for the days ahead. He placed one reed in his mouth, then started bringing the heavy morass of muddy clay up against his body. Soon, nothing but a muddy, eastern wall would show. Aoric prayed to gods he had stopped believing in decades ago that no one would see the reed. He angled it upward to be sure. The shovel shafts rested between his body and his arms like crutches, providing both stability for the long stand ahead, and doubling as weapons and digging utensils if his plan was successful. He would also need their length to assist him with getting out of the tomb, deep as it was.

Aoric couldn't know exactly what happened next, as his hearing was mostly cut off by the clay covering his entire being. The Alan was to raise an alarm to the Hun guarding them, calling him over and making a huge protest that Aoric had crawled out of the hole and abandoned them, running to the south. If the Hun decided to pursue Aoric's alleged course, the Alan would immediately start running north by northeast, to his beloved mountains. If the Hun tried to call for more guards, well, then the Alan was to incapacitate him with the only weapons available – the shovel heads. Secretly, Aoric hoped for this scenario, as it would provide the Alan a fresh horse to escape with, rather than relying on his own sore feet.

After a silence that seemed to stretch into forever, Aoric heard dull, indistinguishable voices from above him, then the distinct thumps of a horse galloping away. *Fly, my friend*, he thought. *Fly and be free.*

You Might Get It

M issy stared at me from across our kitchen table. Every few minutes, an acrid stream of dark fluid dribbled down her chin. Her eyes remained unblinking, her body unmoving.

Missy was unbreathing.

My mother always said *be careful what you wish for, you might get it.* She'd said a lot of foolish things in a life littered with visits to rehab and punctuated by cirrhosis of the liver. She dispensed homespun wisdom the way her furtive purse-digging produced pills. I had never put much stock in either of those ventures. I was starting to invest a little capital in that particular nugget, however.

Mother's voice was annoyed with me for not being more grateful. I envisioned her throwing wrinkled hands up in mock annoyance, then lighting a Virginia Slim; *some people are just chronically dissatisfied.*

I sat at my kitchen table before two of my favorite things in this entire world: a bottle of Canadian whiskey, and Missy...my wife who died just two weeks ago.

She didn't have the presence of mind to say anything other than 'Jih' or 'luh yuh,' which I eventually inferred as analogs for my name, 'Jim,' and 'love you.' I understood why it was difficult for her to speak; death had rendered the muscles of her jaw as tight as piano wire. What bothered me most was that she didn't appear to have the presence *of a mind.*

For my part, I felt I was handling things appropriately. Up until the onset of Missy's stinted pounding at the front door four hours ago, things had progressed naturally. Missy got cancer; I cared for her. She got worse; I started drinking again. She died; I got drunk nightly. If Missy was gone, then my commitment to sobriety could rot as well. My new evening ritual – drinking aside – was to wish and wish and wish until I ground my teeth to the roots that Missy would come back to me. I would wake up alone, covered in sweat or other bodily fluids, around dawn somewhere in our house. I'm sure I made a promise to stop drinking in there, somewhere.

I looked up at Missy from my liquor and let slip a nervous titter. This was *not* what I'd had in mind. She continued to stare at me placidly from across the kitchen table we'd picked out together a decade ago.

My sobriety, similarly acquired ten years ago, was preceded by a hiccup of infidelity on Missy's part in an otherwise smoothly running marriage. Given my late mother's near-constant hints that the presence of a child drains all the joy from one's life, I resolved never to breed. Missy failed to catch my unspoken decision, and five years into our marriage accused me of 'bait-and-switch.' I had no recollection of ever setting the hook, but she insisted that I would often crawl into bed late at night, amorously sloshed, and whisper sweet nothings about wanting to 'procreate the fuck' out of 'her uterus.'

Our clashes were epic, her tears were plentiful and my disengagement was constant. She sought solace in the arms of a swarthy co-worker who referred to me as 'bro' when I confronted them about the affair. The result of the kerfuffle was that she would stay with me on two conditions: that I bear children with her, and that I get sober.

I was successful in one of those endeavors for the ten subsequent years. Missy's diagnosis solved the mystery of why our fervent couplings were not bearing fruit. Her cancer had started in her cervix and then spread, undetected, throughout her body. After a brief, but fierce, battle I surrendered to my disease, after which Missy succumbed to hers.

At least, I thought she had.

Four hours now felt like a lifetime ago. When I answered the slow, arrhythmic pounding on the front door, I slurred an angry "what?" into the face of whoever had dared to interrupt my drinking. Missy stood on the porch, left arm still raised mid-knock, and uttered a guttural whine that shocked me out of my momentary trance.

"Jihhhhhhhhh."

I stepped forward and embraced her, too shocked to register her condition or scent. After a moment, her stiffness alarmed me; did some sick bastard dig my wife up and prop her on my doorstep as a sadistic prank? No, she had spoken, right?

"Missy! I'm so glad you're home!" I released her.

Her neck was canted, her mouth partially open. I considered the position I held a second ago and realized she'd been aiming her teeth at my collarbone. She looked at me dully and her mouth snapped shut. In slow motion, she reverted to an upright posture.

I flipped the switch that turned on the porch light. Missy's skin was grey, a sharp contrast to her yellowed, jaundiced final days. Her hair, a vibrant blonde that shifted during her illness to sandy brown, was now black with mud. Her lips, thin and cracked, seemed too small for her mouth. Her dulled, white teeth showed at all times, resulting in a sustained, farcical grimace. The dress I'd buried her in, a sweet sky-blue sundress that she'd always favored, was filthy and torn at both shoulders. I didn't provide the funeral director with one of her bras, but her panties were around her right ankle. There was no sign of her shoes.

The smell became troublesome to process. A mélange of musky sweetness, earthy loam, chemicals, and outright decay washed over me. I struggled with parallel desires to flee from or further process these scents.

Missy took a halting step forward through the threshold of our home and snapped me out of my own stagnation. I stepped out of her way and closed the door behind her.

"Jihhhhhh. Luh yuh." A hollow version of her voice whined. In the close air of our foyer, any fascination with her scent died.

"Missy," was all I could say. I repeated her name several times, bobbing my head around in an unsuccessful bid to dodge the attack on my nostrils.

I grasped her wrist and pulled lightly to coax her to our bedroom, then through to our master bath. Her steps were slow. I guided her into our shower stall and she was able to step into it easily enough. I turned on the water, initially concerned about the temperature. Hot or cold, Missy didn't appear to care. She stared at me without wavering as the water washed the dirt from her hair. Chunks of mud rested briefly on her yellowed eyeballs, then cascaded down her filthy blue dress to congregate around the center drain. Without thinking, I pulled the dress down over her shoulders, breasts, then hips until it slapped on the floor of the shower. Missy didn't react. I quickly soaped up my hands with her shower gel, then started scrubbing her. Her skin was taut, not hard, but firm. There seemed to be nothing under it but muscle. Her skin remained grey but was at least clean.

I shut off the water, leaned to my right and grabbed a large towel from the rack on the wall, then held it up for her. Missy didn't move, so I stepped partially into the stall and began to wrap the towel around her body. I lifted her arms, guided her through a complete rotation, then cinched the towel edge over her breasts. It hung nearly past her knees. The smell hadn't washed off much. Missy's teeth parted, and her head slowly tilted toward my hands as they worked on the towel. I pulled them away calmly, and Missy's empty teeth clacked together. I lowered her arms again.

My attempt to guide Missy out of the shower resulted in more staring. I tugged gently on her wrists until she stepped out of the stall. I turned her to the left, then forced her to sit on the toilet seat by pressing down on her shoulders. Her body folded accordingly, but as her toweled ass hit the seat, something must have broken inside of her; there was a muffled pop from her lap, followed by a torrent of pink liquid from...somewhere close by. I initially mistook the deluge as blood or other viscera, but once the smell hit, I realized it was red embalming fluid. I staggered backward out of the bathroom, into our bedroom. My left hand covered my mouth and nose.

"Jihhh. Luh yuh." Missy rocked forward in an attempt to stand. When this failed, she began to swing her arms to gain the momentum necessary to rise. This caused me to notice her hands for the first time. Both were demolished; the fingers at droopy, unnatural angles. Most of the nails were missing. On the few that survived, there remained no fingernail polish.

I mean, I told myself, *why don't you try breaking out of that coffin and climbing through five feet of topsoil. Let's see how sexy* you *look.*

This calls for a drink – my mother's favorite pronouncement. More wisdom from beyond the veil. Thanks, Mom.

I guided Missy back to the kitchen and seated her gingerly at our small dinner table. My hand remained on her shoulder for a moment while I stared at the brown paper sack on the kitchen counter; inside, a fresh bottle of whiskey waited. Her head swiveled slowly, and I watched her attempt to bite my index finger. She missed by a few inches, then adjusted her aim and tried again. By then, I'd removed my hand; Missy's motions were comically slow – like she was swimming through gelatin. I went to the counter and grabbed my bottle of whiskey and a tumbler from the cupboard above. I'd long since stopped bothering with ice.

I sat and poured the whiskey, then drained the glass. It burned on the way down, just like I wanted it to. "What am I going to do with you?" I asked.

Missy cocked her head to the left like a puppy. It had the sound of a dry cloth being slowly torn. "Jih?" came haltingly, and that inevitable dark drool sluiced down her blue lips.

I sighed, pouring another smooth gold glassful of one-of-my-two-favorite-things.

"Jihmmmmmmm?"

I couldn't believe it. She said my name...or at least close enough. "Yes? Yes, honey?"

"Luh yuh..."

"Oh, Missy, you don't know how much I love you." Maybe there was hope for her, maybe she just needed to clear the cobwebs out of her head, and day by day she'd get better. "I missed you so much."

"Jihhhhhhmm," she drew out the sound until it ended in a plaintive whine, "*luh* yuh."

A look of annoyance darted across her face. I shuddered, then drained and refilled my glass. *The heart wants what the heart wants,* Mother droned.

Missy was functioning on pure logic, I realized. She loved me. I loved her. I loved her beauty, her voice, her courage in the face of the disease that killed her. She loved human flesh. Why wasn't I returning her love?

I wish this were over. I tipped the glass back, finished it, filled it again and drained it again. I put my head on the table and closed my eyes. *I wish this would end.*

Missy rose; I noticed because it took her several tries to get out of the chair. I didn't move. I swam in my drunken state and pretended it was her when she was alive. Her when she was alive shambling slowly around the table to me. Her towel dropping to the floor in flirtation when she was alive. The scent of rotting hamburger when she was alive. Her when she was alive putting her hands on my shoulders. Her broken wrists and limp, shattered fingers when she was alive. Her when she was alive nibbling playfully on the nape of my neck, gently at first.

At first.

Tuesdays with
Moran'd'arth

S andy Kavanaugh is a deeply unhappy man.
Sandy is also a bestselling author and a millionaire several times
over. He is married to a woman he has loved since college. This woman
bore him two wonderful children and made a home for them all in
pastoral southern Maine. Sandy Kavanaugh owns multiple houses in New

England and a small vacation pad in southern California. He rarely visits any of them.

Despite Sandy's phenomenal success, he is considered a writer of merely average skill within literary circles. Over two dozen of his stories and novels have been developed into television or film projects, with a vast majority being panned as "B movie quality" at best. People recognize his face on the street and often ask for photographs or autographs, both of which he always obliges.

None of these things cause Sandy to be a deeply unhappy man. What makes Sandy truly miserable is the demon under his barn. After more than forty years in thrall to Moran'd'arth, Sandy plans to confront the demon today. This could lead to a horribly painful and prolonged death. As such, Sandy's resolve brings misery spiked with anxiety. But at sixty-three years of age, Sandy feels as though it is time to stand up for himself.

Sandy trudges through the New England snow to the ramshackle barn on the Eastern edge of his rural property. The snow is dry and powdery, and so it flees his steps and whips around on the wind onto his exposed neck. He raises the hood of his heavy coat; with his gloves on, it takes several tries. He is growing frustrated – the shifting winds find a way to deliver snow into every crevice of his outfit. There is no sun in the sky, it seems. There are only clouds to look down on Sandy as his boot sticks in the snow, causing him to put his bootless right foot in the frigid powder. He curses, reverses an unsteady step, and places his numbing foot back into the boot. Melancholy blooms anew within his chest and the world's indifference to it abides.

Upon reaching the barn, Sandy carefully unlocks the several chains that hold the door shut. Their purpose is not to keep Moran'd'arth in, as nothing can keep the demon in or out of anything or anywhere, but to dissuade any interlopers from stumbling into the barn and losing their own soul. Sandy can hardly live with what he did over four decades ago; the idea of someone else doing it due to his carelessness would be unendurable.

Twice yearly he makes this trek – commanded directly by Moran'd'arth. Always on the Tuesday in the first week of February – the anniversary of Sandy's fateful encounter with the demon – to remove remains, and then six months later, on the first Tuesday of August, to bring a sacrifice. That the weather is miserable at both times in New England is coincidental, but it is almost certainly made worse by Sandy's dread at having to face the monster in person. Indeed, it could be warm and perfectly cloudless with no humidity and Sandy's soul would still be desolate.

One August, early in his service to Moran'd'arth, Sandy ignored the psychic directive from the beast for a full day. The next morning he woke to a yard full of dead birds. Not just a few but so many – of varied species – that Sandy could not see grass for a full acre. The blue feathers of robins overlapping the black feathers of crows, which overlapped with the grey feathers of pigeons. A white breast of...some poor fowl shined under the carnage, near the tire swing suspended from the massive oak in the back-yard. And all of their black, glossy eyes stared at him in single-minded, avian judgment. His children howled at the windows in terror, tears dropping onto their pajamas. He tasked his wife with securing the kids and began the cleanup process, lugging dozens of green-black garbage bags into the barn. And after that...

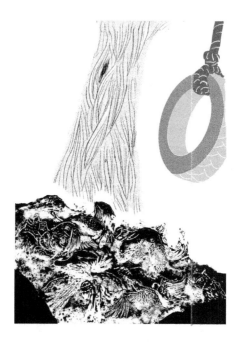

Sandy secures the locks on the inside of the barn door. He pulls off the puffy glove on his right hand and stabs at the smartphone in his left, activating the flashlight. He pans it around the still gloom of the barn. There is nothing in the structure – no rats, not so much as a spider making a home in a high corner of the beams. Nothing living is willing to share space with Moran'd'arth. Nothing except Sandy Kavanaugh, and even he can't bear it any longer. After grabbing an unused burlap bag from a neatly folded pile on the floor, Sandy proceeds down a set of crumbling concrete steps into a chamber beneath the barn. There is a faint musty smell in the air that thickens to an odor far more organic and foul as he descends. Sandy's barn sits over a massive stone cistern that now serves as a basement for the place. He installed the stairs himself decades ago, tired of using a rickety ladder for access.

At the bottom of the steps, in a small six-by-six-foot chamber, Sandy puts his back into moving aside the massive, circular stone at the mouth of the cistern to gain access to Moran'd'arth's cache. For most people, this would conjure an image of the apostles rolling away the stone in front of Jesus's tomb to find it happily empty. Not for Sandy. The bile comes up in his throat; he thinks that he would weep with joy to find this dark niche empty. He steps through the small threshold into the cavernous, dry cistern, pocketing his still illuminated phone.

"Sandy Kavanaugh would surely be dead and decomposing without Moran'd'arth." The demon's voice fills the chamber – and Sandy – with dark reverberation. As has been the case for the past few years, Sandy was not careful to guard his thoughts when near the demon. He clears his mind of all but disgust and fear; these are like food to the creature, but he doesn't mind giving them away.

"Surely, Moran'd'arth." Sandy goes down to one knee, the patella finding a painful pebble to rest on with classic accuracy. Sandy waits for the demon to begin his usual admonition, reminding Sandy that it was *he* who sought out the demon and begged Moran'd'arth to provide *him* with wealth and fame, not the other way around. Sandy needs no reminders, as the demon well knows. Every dollar Sandy spends on something, from a packet of gum to a sports car, weighs heavily on his tattered soul.

Instead, Moran'd'arth – still shrouded in pitch darkness – merely begins the agonizingly slow process of regurgitating the skeleton of the sacrifice Sandy brought him last summer. Fortunately, this year it is simply the remains of a fattened pig that Sandy had raised from a piglet. It could be far worse; in the years before Sandy locked the barn doors, Moran'd'arth lured the occasional human to this lair. Once or twice, Sandy has been forced to provide the demon with a runaway or hitchhiker or other such lost soul. Indeed, back in 1993, a desperate Sandy Kavanaugh threw an overzealous fan into its maw. The fan of Sandy's books had managed to stalk the writer to his home, and when the young man wouldn't leave peacefully on that early August day, Sandy killed two birds with a Louisville slugger-shaped stone.

The wet smacks and deep, bass-heavy rumbles end after what feels like a half-hour. The smell of a stale pond full of dead amphibians wells off the creature. It has soaked into the stone walls and earthen floor of the cavern. Sandy still has the indignity of loading the pig's remains into the burlap sack to come. He rises.

A torch bursts into flame a few inches to the right of Sandy's head. Despite this being the monster's ritual – only lighting the chamber once it has given the bones back – this never fails to make Sandy jump to the opposite wall in surprise. A sound like gravel being crushed emanates from the demon; Sandy has always understood this as the creature's version of laughter. He lifts his left foot from where it has landed and sees the crushed porcine skull underneath. Sandy moves back to the right, to the center of the chamber.

"Moran'd'arth commands Sandy Kavanaugh's attention."

"Sandy Kavanaugh's attention is Moran'd'arth's." Once, Sandy had made the mistake of using a different form of address to the demon – something like 'master' or some other sniveling form of verbal supplication. Moran'd'arth had whipped out a tentacle and bloodied the flesh of Sandy's bare bicep. For Moran'd'arth, and for the rest of Moran'd'arth's kind, Sandy reckoned, using a being's proper name was not only fitting but reverent. That Moran'd'arth referred to Sandy by his full name at least confirmed it was appropriate; Moran'd'arth was reverent to no one but Moran'd'arth.

"Sandy Kavanaugh has served Moran'd'arth adequately for many of Sandy Kavanaugh's years. Moran'd'arth has provided Sandy Kavanaugh with what Sandy Kavanaugh asked. Moran'd'arth commands that Sandy Kavanaugh continue to provide Moran'd'arth with sacrifices and the sacrifices' removal until Sandy Kavanaugh no longer lives, but is rotting in the earth or within Moran'd'arth."

This gives Sandy great pause. He had always hoped that the creature would avoid killing him, but now, he is no longer sure. It also flies directly in the face of what Sandy wanted to ask of the devil: release from their pact.

Reading these thoughts, Moran'd'arth thunders, "SANDY KAVANAUGH WILL DO AS MORAN'D'ARTH COMMANDS, NOT AS SANDY KAVANAUGH WISHES. MORAN'D'ARTH HAS GIVEN SANDY KAVANAUGH PRECISELY WHAT SANDY KAVANAUGH BARGAINED FOR. SANDY KAVANAUGH'S FAME IS SUCH THAT ALMOST EVERY HUMAN IN THIS WORLD KNOWS THE NAME OF SANDY KAVANAUGH. SANDY KAVANAUGH HAS MORE WEALTH THAN SANDY KAVANAUGH CAN USE IN SEVERAL PATHETIC LIFETIMES."

Sandy swiftly prostrates himself before the indignant demon, whose singular eye has darkened in anger. Sandy looks up from his prone position on the dirt floor, his hands covering his ears, and takes in the full horror of Moran'd'arth.

Moran'd'arth is a greenish-blue-black round mass of goo at least twelve feet high and eight feet in circumference. Its main feature is a solitary, massive and lidless yellow eye set amid the terrifying morass of tentacles and viscous fluid. There is a small mouth south of the eye, but this is only opened when feeding or vomiting; the creature does not speak from this orifice. Sandy has never counted the tentacles. He knows only that they are legion, and that they are sharp. Sandy posits that Moran'd'arth is like an iceberg, in that there is much, much more of the beast below the ground. He'd glimpsed underneath Moran'd'arth once, in fact, when Sandy brought down the manic, struggling stalker-fan in '93.

Upon being dragged into Moran'd'arth's chamber, the idiot awoke and viciously head-butted Sandy, then attempted to run. Lying on his left side, on the floor of the cistern, Sandy saw Moran'd'arth lift his visible bulk to lunge after the screaming man. Sandy spied tentacles under the monster that widened dramatically the further they went into the earth, like the roots of a mighty tree. At that moment, Sandy's mind conjured an image of Moran'd'arth's root system traversing hundreds of miles of earthy loam, deep under the water table. The tentacles pushed through rock like a fork through cake. Moran'd'arth had likely caused Sandy's mind to descry the enormity of Moran'd'arth's being; there was no other explanation for it beyond simple imagination. Sandy had stopped believing in his imagination long before that terrible day.

Moran'd'arth snagged the fleeing sacrifice with its outstretched tentacles, settled its bulk down with a boom of wet flatulence, and slowly pulled the screaming stalker into its mouth. The eating went on for hours. The shrieks only lasted about forty-five minutes. Sandy watched it all.

Now, Moran'd'arth continues in a tone a few decibels lower. "If Moran'd'arth wills that Sandy Kavanaugh is the final sacrifice that Sandy Kavanaugh is responsible for bringing to Moran'd'arth, then that is what Sandy Kavanaugh's demise shall be."

As he speaks, Sandy returns to his kneeling position. "Yes, Moran'd'arth's will be done."

Moran'd'arth settles into a more conversational tone. "Of course Moran'd'arth's will be done – what other will could there possibly be? Sandy Kavanaugh came to Moran'd'arth forty-three of Sandy Kavanaugh's years ago and begged Moran'd'arth for success as a writer and great wealth. Moran'd'arth knew that Sandy Kavanaugh would not achieve either without the help of Moran'd'arth, and so Moran'd'arth bargained with Sandy Kavanaugh. Moran'd'arth has held up Moran'd'arth's side of this accord."

It is now or never to plead his case, Sandy surmises. "Mighty Moran'd'arth—" he flinches at the inclusion of this adjective, but the demon's tentacles merely twitch rather than strike out at him— "is wise and powerful and eternal. Moran'd'arth's servant is growing older, weaker. Possibly infirm. Sandy Kavanaugh's physicians suspect that Sandy Kavanaugh might have a cancerous polyp in Sandy Kavanaugh's colon –"

"Moran'd'arth knows this and all things."

"Yes, indeed Moran'd'arth does. Given that Sandy Kavanaugh's health might soon prohibit him, er, Sandy Kavanaugh, from being able to, ah, procure sacrifices and serve Moran'd'arth...?" Sandy lets the question hang in the fetid air.

Moran'd'arth stays silent. In fact, all visible movement ceases.

Sandy does not see the monster's idle tentacles as resting so much as poised to strike, like serpents. Mentally wincing, he continues. "Would Moran'd'arth be willing to release Sandy Kavanaugh from Moran'd'arth's service? Not for the benefit of Sandy Kavanaugh," he adds quickly, "but to ensure the continued...edification...of Moran'd'arth's grandeur."

"Sandy Kavanaugh is not using that word – edification – correctly. Sandy Kavanaugh's peers are correct in assuming Sandy Kavanaugh is nearly illiterate." Moran'd'arth is also given to reminding Sandy of his shortcomings usually once per visit. At least this time the demon does not wax poetic about the inadequacy of Sandy's penis, as the demon has gleaned from the mind of Sandy's wife and reported to him multiple times over the years.

"Apologies, Moran'd'arth. Sandy Kavanaugh's question remains before Moran'd'arth's greatness."

The demon's tentacles begin swaying randomly. "If Sandy Kavanaugh is not in service to Moran'd'arth, then Sandy Kavanaugh is dead. If Sandy Kavanaugh wishes to leave this chamber alive, unconsumed, then Sandy Kavanaugh will continue to serve Moran'd'arth."

"Y-yes, Moran'd'arth," Sandy mumbles. He briefly considers snatching up the torch and jamming it into the massive eye of the creature. The eye is always connected to the brain—is this not so for all earthbound creatures? There must be a way to kill this thing and find release.

Again, Moran'd'arth's tentacles freeze, poised in the thick air, their tips pointing directly at Sandy. Sandy freezes as well. The only movement in the chamber is the sweat dripping from Sandy's sideburns, down his cheeks, and the rising and falling of his chest. Minutes pass. Sandy's peripheral vision is fixed on the hypnotic flickering of the torch.

"Moran'd'arth will give Sandy Kavanaugh a second gift," the demon voices in a tone the writer has not heard before, an almost caring, soft voice that stuns Sandy.

"Thank you, mighty Mor-" Sandy's sniveling is cut short as a group of Moran'd'arth's tentacles shoot out, embedding their tips in the stones behind him. Two of them have drawn blood – one from his right cheek and the other from his left trapezius. Goose down from the ripped collar of his jacket floats in the thick air. Sandy has the good sense to remain still; *if this is the end, then it will be over in an hour or two,* he thinks.

"No, Sandy Kavanaugh, this is not the end. Moran'd'arth offers Sandy

Kavanaugh a new bargain. In exchange for Sandy Kavanaugh's continued service, Moran'd'arth will not cause what Sandy Kavanaugh terms 'forensic evidence' to come into the possession of the police of this region. Sandy Kavanaugh will not be implicated in dozens of murders, Sandy Kavanaugh's family will not be made insolvent and homeless, and Sandy Kavanaugh will not be consumed by Moran'd'arth. Instead, Sandy Kavanaugh will continue to serve Moran'd'arth throughout the course of Sandy Kavanaugh's colon cancer, for cancer is what Sandy Kavanaugh already has. Sandy Kavanaugh will continue to bring sacrifices to Moran'd'arth even after the disease spreads to Sandy Kavanaugh's liver and lymph nodes, eventually metastasizing in Sandy Kavanaugh's brain. Sandy Kavanaugh will die a painful, lingering death in two of Sandy Kavanaugh's years' time,"

Sandy stands unmoving, the cold dread of truth washing down his spine.

"Or Moran'd'arth will consume Sandy Kavanaugh on this very day, at this very hour, in such a way that will make Sandy Kavanaugh's suffering through cancer seem like the orgasmic culmination of sexual coupling." The tentacles retract, slicing through several other locations on Sandy's body on their way back to the demon.

Before Sandy can answer one way or another – as if such a decision is needed – the beast's entire form shudders. The ground shakes enough for the pig's skeleton to clatter apart, reminding Sandy he has not bagged it up yet. The torch vibrates out of its holder and falls to the floor. Sandy hesitates before finally picking up the torch and placing it back in the depression dug into the wall for it. The last time he saw Moran'd'arth react this way, there had been a particularly horrific school shooting—the one in Florida, Sandy recalls. Certainly, something terrible has happened somewhere, and the demon's limbs have gleaned the fear, resentment, guilt, and suffering from the world like a human takes in air. Moran'd'arth was not this large in the 1980s. The monster has doubled in size in the last decade alone, but Sandy doesn't like to think too much about this. Sandy hopes the cancer will finish him before the monster outgrows the cellar.

Sandy begins envisioning the creation of a charity into which he can funnel most of his wealth. Of course, his wife and adult daughters will be taken care of for the rest of their lives. He will stipulate that this property be sold, and that this barn...no, best not to actively think of it. Sandy struggles not to think of trucks and concrete and cleansing fire.

"Sandy Kavanaugh may leave Moran'd'arth's presence now." A grating sound echoes around the chamber, hurting Sandy's ears. "Sandy Kavanaugh's schemes against Moran'd'arth will come to naught. Remember that Moran'd'arth has given Sandy Kavanaugh a great gift today, and Moran'd'arth can revoke this gift. Sandy Kavanaugh can always suffer more greatly. Now, leave Moran'd'arth."

Sandy flees the chamber, then the barn, utterly forgetting to collect the porcine bones. He stumbles into the house, breathing heavily. He shucks his coat, gloves and boots, then drinks himself completely drunk inside of thirty minutes. He does not answer his wife's questions about why he is suddenly day drinking. He has two years to keep this terrible, terrible secret. Only two years left.

Sandy weeps with joy for the first time in his long life, then passes out in his recliner before lunchtime.

K'CETNOC & THE ETERNAL JOURNEY, PART 2: THERAPY

"**K**'CETNOC IS UNSURE THAT K'CETNOC SHOULD BE IN A RELATIONSHIP AT THIS TIME."

Rosalind Greenbaum, a fifty-two-year-old therapist specializing in trauma, leaned back in her leather office chair. A pen was poised at her lips; she tended to chew it while seeing the lithoid being who frequented her office every Tuesday from three to four p.m. "Hmmm."

"WHAT DOES DOCTOR GREENBAUM THINK ABOUT K'CETNOC'S RELATIONSHIP?"

In her own therapy, with her colleague and former lover Sidney Truesdale, Rosalind remarked that the massive rock-being's visits brought up her old habit of chewing. Pens, fingernails, the flesh adjacent to her thumbnail; these all fell victim to this tendency. She often became angry with Sidney during their exchanges about K'cetnoc, because Sidney refused to believe that Rosalind was providing therapy to a literal timeless being made entirely of rocks. He invariably raised an eyebrow in lewd suggestion and posited that Ros must have some sort of oral fixation triggered by interaction with the brute.

"DOCTOR GREENBAUM?"

Rosalind cut short a daydream about tipping Sidney's office chair over – with him in it – using her outstretched toes. "I'm sorry, K'cetnoc. You're referring to your...*relationship*...with Bambi?"

"BRITTANI."

"Brittani, yes, sorry. A relationship is a two-way street, K'cetnoc. Are you sure this 'Brittani' shares your feelings?"

"THIS RELATIONSHIP IS NOT A THOROUGHFARE. UNLESS DOCTOR GREENBAUM IS ALSO USING A COLLO-QUIALISM RELYING ON ROAD-BASED METAPHOR."

"Yes, K'cetnoc, I think –"

"BRITTANI HAS TOLD K'CETNOC NUMEROUS TIMES THAT BRITTANI IS K'CETNOC'S COMPANION, AND THAT K'CETNOC IS BRITTANI'S."

Rosalind began to speak but stopped herself. She was about to remind the being sitting cross-legged in the center of her office, the better to spare her furniture, that her practice specialized in traumas suffered during workplace violence, natural disasters, et cetera. K'cetnoc did not seem to understand the distinction between how he felt and how someone who'd had a building collapse on them felt. She once advised him that one of her patients had been trapped next to the bleeding body of a co-worker for six hours before the active shooter stalking through her workplace had been killed by police. K'cetnoc told her that he agreed with her assessment, that how K'cetnoc felt was very much akin to how her patient must have felt.

He decreed that Dr. Greenbaum was the perfect choice to assist in his therapy, seeing as how she had just summed up his feelings so succinctly.

Instead, Rosalind decided to take a different approach. Rather than her telling this rocky being that he was clearly being led on by a hot young twenty-something, Rosalind would lead him to make his own conclusion. "K'cetnoc, when was the last time you were in a relationship? Let's see if we can find a thread from one of your past-"

"K'CETNOC HAS BEEN IN MANY RELATIONSHIPS. SOME OF THEM PREDATE THE ATMOSPHERE OF THIS WORLD."

"Well, we don't need to parse every one of them." She tried to head off the lapidarian creature's reverie.

"K'CETNOC FIRST FELL IN LOVE WITH WHAT HUMANS CALL ARCHAEA, WHICH CAME BEFORE WHAT HUMANS CALL BACTERIA."

"I hardly see how you could carry on a serious-"

"THIS ARCHAEA WAS STUNNING. IT HAD A DEPTH OF FEELING THAT NONE OF THE OTHER TRILLIONS OF ITS BRETHEREN WERE CAPABLE OF."

"Oookay." Rosalind set her legal pad down and put the plunger of her ballpoint into her mouth.

"THIS ARCHAEA WAS GRACEFUL. EVERY DECISION IT MADE WAS LIKE A SYMPHONY IN MOTION. 'MOVE' IT WOULD THINK, AND THEN IT WOULD MOVE. 'EAT' IT WOULD THINK, AND THEN IT WOULD ABSORB ANOTHER SMALLER PROKARYOTE. 'SUBDIVIDE' IT WOULD THINK, AND THEN-"

"K'cetnoc," Rosalind gently interrupted, "I think I get the idea."

"YES, OF COURSE. THIS ARCHAEA'S BEAUTY WAS SUCH THAT K'CETNOC SCARCELY NEED BOTHER DESCRIBING IT. DOCTOR GREENBAUM UNDERSTANDS FULLY. THE RELATIONSHIP ENDED TRAGICALLY WHEN THE ATMOSPHERE OF THIS PLANET CHANGED FROM NITROGEN AND CARBON DIOXIDE TO PREDOMINATELY OXYGEN."

"That must have been very difficult for you." Rosalind intoned, now flicking through her smartphone.

"K'CETNOC HAS HAD MANY RELATIONSHIPS OVER THE MILLENNIA. TARDIGRADES, OR WHAT HUMANS CALL 'WATER-BEARS.' A PROMINENT CONSERVATIVE SENATOR FROM THE SOUTHERN UNITED STATES. AN ENTIRE ENCLAVE OF POISON DART FROGS IN THE JUNGLES OF THAILAND. SEVERAL DOUGLAS FIRS. CYANOBACTERIA. A PRECURSOR TO THE WOLVERINE DURING THE EARLY CENOZOIC. RUSSIANS."

"It seems as though you target the emotionally unavailable with unerring accuracy."

K'cetnoc either ignored or silently acknowledged this. It was impossible for her to know.

"K'CETNOC WOULD LIKE TO TELL DOCTOR GREEN-BAUM ABOUT A PARTICULARLY PAINFUL RELATIONSHIP."

Rosalind put aside her sarcasm, touched by the vulnerability in K'cetnoc's craggy voice. She nodded.

"THIS HAPPENED MILLIONS OF YEARS AGO, DURING WHAT HUMANS CALL THE CRETACEOUS PERIOD."

Rosalind's face scrunched slightly, and she gave a tight smile that indicated *of course it was, go on.*

"K'CETNOC LIVED IN A CAVE WITH TWO INDIVIDUALS THAT HUMANS WOULD DESCRIBE AS HADROSAURS. THESE WERE A BONDED PAIR. WE HAPPENED UPON EACH OTHER AT A WATER SITE. THE HADROSAURS WERE DRINKING, AND K'CETNOC WAS GATHERING MATERIAL TO K'CETNOC. K'CETNOC HAD RECENTLY SUFFERED AN INJURY WHICH HAD REDUCED K'CETNOC'S MASS BY ONE-QUARTER."

Rosalind twirled the index finger of her right hand, indicating that K'cetnoc should proceed with the tale.

"K'CETNOC DOES NOT NEED TO DESCRIBE TO DOCTOR GREENBAUM THE SORT OF ATTRACTION THAT FROZE THE THREE OF US AT THAT MOMENT. DOCTOR GREENBAUM HAS EXPERIENCED LOVE AT FIRST SIGHT, CERTAINLY."

K'cetnoc didn't give Rosalind long to consider this. Apparently, the being assumed that love at first sight was a common thing; it certainly seemed to be for K'cetnoc. Rosalind's memory drifted, unbidden, to a night six years ago at the Boston Logan Airport Marriott during an industry conference. There had been too much white wine, and Rosalind had locked gazes with a handsome colleague across the darkened buffet. She recalled furtively sliding her wedding and engagement rings off her finger and into her purse...

"AS K'CETNOC INDICATED EARLIER, THE HADROSAURS WERE A BONDED PAIR. THEY HAD NOT BEEN ABLE TO SUCCESSFULLY FERTILIZE THE FEMALE'S EGGS. THE THREE OF US BECAME LOVERS IN THAT CAVE, WHICH OVERLOOKED WHAT HUMANS NOW CALL OKLA-HOMA CITY. OUR TIME TOGETHER WAS TORRID, EACH EXPLORING THE OTHER'S BODIES WITH PASSIONATE ABANDON..."

"Jesus Christ," Rosalind remarked, pulled from her own memories into the consideration of a prehistoric threesome.

"AFTER WHAT SEEMED LIKE YEARS, THE FEMALE HADROSAUR LAID A CLUTCH OF EGGS. A SHORT PERIOD LATER, THREE TINY HATCHLINGS EMERGED FROM THE NEST. THE HADROSAURS WERE ECSTATIC. K'CETNOC TRIED TO SHARE IN THEIR JOY, BUT IT BECAME IMMEDI-ATELY APPARENT THAT K'CETNOC WAS NO LONGER WELCOME IN THEIR HOME."

Despite herself, Rosalind frowned. "Aw."

"IN K'CETNOC'S HEARTBREAK AND DESPAIR, K'CETNOC DID NOT WARN THE HADROSAURS OF THE METEOROID WHICH WAS ABOUT TO COLLIDE WITH EARTH, IN WHAT HUMANS NOW REFER TO AS 'THE GULF OF MEXICO.'"

Rosalind's mouth fell open.

"PLEASE DO NOT JUDGE K'CETNOC, DOCTOR GREEN-BAUM. K'CETNOC IS NOT PROUD OF K'CETNOC'S JEALOUSY."

After a period of stunned silence, Rosalind remembered her duty. "K'cetnoc, certainly there was nothing you could have done to prevent this cataclysm, right?"

The rocky being remained silent, concentrating on his massive, stony hands.

"Right??" she repeated, concern causing her voice to rise.

"K'CETNOC DOES NOT CONTROL BOLLIDES WHICH MIGRATE FROM THE OUTER SOLAR SYSTEM TO BECOME ENSNARED BY THIS PLANET'S GRAVITY."

Rosalind sensed the tiniest hint of derision in K'cetnoc's voice. "Moving on. What can you say that you've learned from each of these... many, many relationships, K'cetnoc?"

"THAT K'CETNOC IS DOOMED TO BE ALONE AND UNHAPPY."

"I think that's a valid feeling, K'cetnoc. Most people have definitely felt that way at one time or another. If you're honest with your partner or...*partners*...then that in turn paves the way for success in a relationship." Rosalind forced a smile at the dejected elemental on her office floor. "The person you're in a relationship with should be someone who will protect your heart."

"DOCTOR GREENBAUM THINKS THAT BRITTANI WILL BE THE ONE TO PROTECT K'CETNOC'S HEART, THEN?"

"Well, I didn't say that exactly."

Seizing on her hesitation, K'cetnoc sprung to his full height. His head poked through one of the acoustic ceiling tiles, raining white dust upon his brow. Her diploma from Yale fell off the south wall with a clatter.

"K'CETNOC CANNOT THANK DOCTOR GREENBAUM ENOUGH. THIS IS THE VALIDATION THAT K'CETNOC HAS BEEN SEARCHING FOR SINCE MEETING BRITTANI AT CLUB RIO. K'CETNOC'S TIME IS UP, AND K'CETNOC MUST GO TO BRITTANI TO TELL BRITTANI HOW K'CETNOC REALLY FEELS.'

Rosalind's hands went to her mouth. "Oh, dear."

"THANK YOU, DOCTOR. K'CETNOC WILL MAIL A CHECK TO COVER WHAT DOCTOR GREENBAUM CALLS 'THE CO-PAY.' K'CETNOC WILL ENDEAVOR NOT TO DAMAGE DOCTOR GREENBAUM'S DOOR ON K'CETNOC'S WAY OUT THIS TIME."

With that, the massive granite creature awkwardly fit his head, then shoulders, then the rest of his bulk through Rosalind's office door. She heard his footfalls for a good two minutes after.

By the time those faded, she had a scotch on the rocks in her left hand and the flesh of her right thumb between her teeth. She chewed, staring through her window at the autumn Connecticut foliage surrounding her office park, and idly swirled the ice around in the tumbler, making it clink.

PLANDEMIC

"Ahhhh, this is what these old bones needed," sighed the one with platinum blonde hair as he dropped his frame into the chaise lounge.

The one with the dark brown hair smiled slyly at his friend and eased himself into his own seat, being careful to avoid spilling his drink as he did so. "Oh, let it be known that on January 18th of this, the year of our...well, me...two thousand and nineteen, that you were actually happy with a decision I made, for once."

"Oh, stow that shit, we're on vacation." Light Hair said, his eyes already closed against the midday sun. He reached for his own drink, which he'd set on a small glass-topped table next to his chair. After a long sip through the cardboard straw and a wince at the taste, he asked, "Where did you book us for vacation this year? I didn't even pay attention."

Dark Hair gingerly tested his own drink and answered around the ice cube in his mouth, "Mauritius."

"Mauritius. Where the hell is—"

"Middle of the Indian Ocean. East of Madagascar. 'Bout thirty-six hundred miles West of Perth, Australia."

"Oh, yeah, that's right. Sweet."

"I mean, sure, unless the Sumatra-Andaman subduction zone acts up, in which case these gorgeous bodies we've chosen will wash up in the Seychelles in about a week."

Light Hair turned his head slowly and gave a withering stare.

Dark Hair smiled. "Just kidding. Nothing scheduled. But, you know..." He gave a playful shrug. "Geology."

Light Hair returned to his drink and finally lost patience with the flavor. "What am I drinking here? This tastes like...France."

Dark Hair smiled again. "Called a Green Tiki Monk. Pineapple syrup, coconut butter rum, and absinthe, apparently."

Light Hair frowned. "Irony aside, that's just wrong...I thought we were going to get along on this vacation?"

Dark Hair's face feigned innocence. "We are! You don't like it?"

"Okay, how many years have we been doing this? No, don't answer, that was a rhetorical question. You know I hate pineapple. Hawaii, 1992. Ring a bell?"

Dark Hair made a show of thinking for a moment. "Oh, Typhoon Iniki!"

"Uh huh. And you know I hate rum. Absolutely despise it. Most of the reason we're not sitting in the Caribbean right now. And absinthe..."

Dark Hair could no longer hide his mischievous glee and burst into laughter. He reached over and attempted to slap the forearm of his companion, but Light Hair moved his arm and fixed his mouth in a pout.

"You know it's no coincidence that Absinthe and the French Revolution arrived at roughly the same time..."

"I'll get you another." Dark Hair's face was sincere. "I mean, a different drink. What do you want?"

"What are you drinking?"

"It's called a 'Sunrise.' It's like a Tequila Sunrise but has rum instead."

"What do they have without rum in it?"

Dark Hair thought for a moment. "Water?"

"Son of a bitch." Light Hair whipped his head around to his left, then his right, scanning for the location of the beachfront bar. He gave Dark Hair a pouty but gentle glare before awkwardly rising from his reclined beach chair and stalking away through the sand.

Dark Hair giggled gaily to himself, then took another sip from his drink. It was so easy to get under the other one's skin that he had to devise more complex and entertaining ways to do it nowadays. He nestled more deeply into the chaise lounge and took in the amazing panorama of creation on display at this beach, the exclusive property of the *Shangri-La Le Touessrok*. Pleasure boats of varying sizes streaked across the turquoise waters. The sea met the sand.

The sand.

His mind drifted to something he'd said a long time ago. To whom had he said it? Oh, yes, Jeremiah. *I will make their widows more numerous than the sand of the sea.* Threats and promises. Prophecies and politics. The destruction of Jerusalem's temple.

Well, they'd been warned. Say what they might about his "mysterious ways," he'd telegraphed his feelings pretty succinctly back then. Back when subtlety was practically pointless.

Things were starting to edge that way again...

"Beer. Can you believe that?" Light Hair was back, a brown bottle held between two fingers of his right hand, interrupting his friend from an ever-darkening reverie. "I might as well have just asked for water."

"Yeah, if you want to spend most of this vacation on the toilet, sure." Dark Hair still stared out into the sea, his voice a little distant despite the sarcasm.

They passed a few minutes in silence, and then Light Hair spoke up, his anger faded. "You're not getting melancholy again, are you? I know that look on your face, even if it's a borrowed one."

"What look? Piss off."

"Oh, yes. Yes, yes, yes. You're taking another one of your dangerous trips down memory lane, aren't you?"

Dark Hair had one hand resting on the arm of the lounger, holding his sweating drink, the other hand casually behind his head in a perfectly composed facsimile of relaxation. Light Hair's entire posture was pointed toward his friend, practically threatening to tip his own chaise lounge over.

Light Hair elected for patience.

"It's just that they're so fucking smug about things now, right?" Dark Hair finally said, his voice controlled but close to gaining volume.

"I know."

"Every single time I leave them to their own devices, they forget I exist.

They forget everything that I've given them. They..." Dark Hair's voice trailed off.

"They don't realize all you've done for them." Light Hair filled in the unspoken line.

Dark Hair grunted.

"Look, we've had this discussion several times. You've given them something so amazing, so perfect, that they can't help but forget about where it came from and just enjoy it. And yes, in enjoying it, they take it for granted."

"Take it for granted." Dark Hair repeated the words with a snarl. His right hand gently turned the glass in place. Drops of water fled his touch and pooled where the glass made contact with the plastic of the lounger's arm.

Light Hair winced. An explosion was imminent.

"DO YOU HAVE," Dark Hair started loudly, then caught himself and continued in a more civilized tone. "Any idea how badly they're damaging what I've created for them?"

"You know I do," Light Hair replied patiently.

"And they've set their sights on other planets now. It's not enough that they need to fuck this one up, but now they've got plans to fuck up several other creations!"

Light Hair reached over to pat Dark Hair's forearm, but it was still crooked behind his head, so he simply patted the left arm of the chaise lounge instead. "Fucking Elon, am I right?" Light Hair tried to inject some levity into the conversation. He needed to steer Dark Hair out of these emotional stormy waters before they were seated in front of literal ones.

"Oh, don't get me started on that little prick..." Dark Hair finally looked over at Light Hair. He saw the smile on his friend's face and returned it, faintly. "Don't worry, I'm not going to..."

"Going to what?" Light Hair asked playfully.

"You know. *Smite them.*" Dark Hair said in a sing-song voice, mocking himself.

"Look, if you want my opinion –" Light Hair hesitated. "– and you *do* actually want my opinion, right?"

Dark Hair was looking at him now, searching his eyes for something. He nodded once.

Light Hair continued. "Look, they're overdue for a good smiting. I'll be the first to admit it. And I know that you think I...what's the word? *Mollycoddle* them."

"I don't think anyone has used that word in two hundred years, but sure," Dark Hair said drily.

"Whatever. I have a long history of taking their side. No two ways about it. We don't need to hash it out again. But you're correct in feeling they've forgotten the divine. The mystical. Something larger than themselves."

Dark Hair looked out toward the waters of the Indian Ocean again. "They don't think there *is* anything larger than themselves."

"Right, my point exactly. So, do I want you to hurt them? No, of course not. That's my entire M.O. But do I want to be forgotten? To be scorned as a fairy tale or worse, be blamed for their society collapsing? Absolutely not. I'm not even the thing they're afraid of any longer. It's something called *The Illuminati* and...fucking...*lizard people*." Light Hair trailed off.

Dark Hair was looking at Light Hair again, his eyebrows raised in appreciation of how impassioned his companion's speech had become.

"I don't want them *all* smote, I guess is what I'm saying." Light Hair resumed his reclined position on the lounge chair, his gaze going past the distant ocean waves.

"Right. No worldwide flood." Dark Hair was looking at the same horizon.

"Right. No asteroids. Just...something to make them stop worshipping the almighty dollar."

"Oh, I'm with you there." Dark Hair moved his drink to his left hand and tipped it toward Light Hair's direction. "I don't even need them to worship me. Not right now, at least. Just that they stop worshipping celebrities, athletes, and...fucking currency."

"Amen." Light Hair clinked his bottle against Dark Hair's glass, and their eyes met. "Got anything specific in mind?"

Dark Hair moved his jaw in contemplation, his lips puckering a bit.

"I've got something that's been around for a while, sort of lurking. We tested it out a few years ago."

"Oh? Anything I had a hand in?"

"No, no." Dark Hair shook his head gently. "We threw it at the birds. It got beta-tested in Asia quite a bit."

"Ohhhhhhh, I think I know what you're talking about." Light Hair nodded knowingly. "Delivery system this time around?"

"I'm thinking of really throwing them a curve. Some wacky combination of, like, a bat and a pangolin. Or something ridiculous like that."

"That sounds like the beginning of a terrible joke."

"You're telling me." Dark Hair drained the rest of his drink in one huge draught and slapped the glass on the table next to him. "Ahhh! You drunk enough to go fuck yet?"

"I thought you'd never ask." Light Hair polished off his beer, again rose unsteadily with his feet astride the chaise lounge, then followed Dark Hair across the sand and into their room at the Shangri-La.

BIZARRE LOVE TRIANGLE

A RETELLING OF THE THREE BEARS

Barry grunted against the stubborn deadbolt of his summer home. For whatever reason, it had been on the fritz ever since he'd bought the place, regardless of how much lubricant he sprayed into it. His frustration was mounting. The two full sacks of groceries in his arms didn't make the process any easier.

Ursula, Barry's wife of twenty-six years, sighed as if *she* were the only one the door was thwarting. Barry started to rumble a sarcastic response, but then the key finally turned to the right and the deadbolt unlocked.

Bruno, Ursula and Barry's son, trundled in behind his sweaty parents, then turned and locked the deadbolt. Barry saw this from the corner of his eye as he gingerly set the grocery bags on the counter, but the pre-teen was off and down the hall to his room before Barry could bark out an admonishment. Bruno's new habit of locking all doors behind himself had resulted in several angry phone calls from Barry to Ursula, telling her that he needed to be let back into the house after checking the post, putting out the garbage bins, sneaking a fag, etcetera. It was really starting to get Barry's hackles up.

Ursula distracted him by continuing her line of questioning from the hour-long drive, one that Barry was not keen to continue. "I just can't understand how something can vanish from your office. If you didn't fancy it, Baz, you could've just told us."

Barry placed his hands flat on the counter and stared at them, trying to keep his voice level. "Swear down, Lulu, my love, the frame was there the last time I was at the office, two days ago."

This was true. The frame in question had been an anniversary gift from Ursula. It was a nondescript rectangular frame which, when a USB thumb drive was plugged into the side of it, would cycle through the various photo files contained on the drive. She'd insisted that Barry keep it on his desk at his office. Barry found it maddeningly distracting, as the change in photos every fifteen seconds was a jarring bit of motion in his peripheral vision. Ursula explained that the twenty-sixth wedding anniversary gift was supposed to be art, and what better art to adorn his desk than a collection of pictures of his loving family?

Fookin' owt, Barry thought at the time, but had smiled and hugged his wife and thanked her for the gift. He promised to put it right on his work desk. And that's where the bloody thing had been two nights ago, during a particularly frenetic session of fellatio from the office's new cleaning girl. Barry knew this for sure, as he'd had to turn the frame face down because it was distracting him then, too.

"If you say so..." Ursula's voice trailed off as she went through to their suite of bedrooms, her tone that of someone who distinctly did not believe what had been said.

Barry finished putting away the groceries, then slumped into the easy chair in the small living room. It had been a hot, boring drive east from Manchester on the A57, past Glossop to here. Ursula wouldn't have even known about the missing gift if he hadn't been forced to stop at his office to retrieve the keys to the home. Despite Barry telling them both to stay in the car, Ursula and Bruno had trundled upstairs behind him, Ursula eyeing the place for...Heaven knows what, really, Bruno undoubtedly looking for things to lock.

Barry had purchased this vacation home three years prior and made every attempt to use it as much as possible since, but the lack of care was clear. Cobwebs shrouded each corner of the ceiling, and there was a musty smell emanating from...somewhere. At least the tiny "panic room" was clean; no one had been in there since he bought the place. Why the previous owners had sacrificed a bedroom for such a thing—out in the country, even—Barry would Barry would never understand. He craned his neck to see into the backyard through the French doors, and the weeds were nearly as tall as his barbeque grill.

Rather than do anything about it, Barry cranked back the reclining chair and promptly fell asleep.

Forty minutes later, Ursula woke Barry with the characteristic *tsk tsk* sound she made whenever he dared to nap. Why the woman couldn't stand the idea of him relaxed, he might never learn.

"It's almost time for supper, luv," Ursula called behind her while heading into the kitchen. "I'll get the table set. Can you start grilling the sirloins?"

Barry growled an affirmative in her direction. It turned to a groan as he hefted his fifty-year-old bulk from the recliner. While retrieving the steaks from Ursula, she reminded him that there was still no cellular signal out here on her mobile phone. "That's the point, *luv*. To get away from all that shite." He managed a half-hearted smile.

Ursula frowned in his direction.

His smile dropped. "It's been like this for three years, Lulu. It's not likely to change." Barry stalked away and began grilling the steaks.

Getting Bruno to abandon his computer in favor of dinner was a constant challenge. Barry was in no mood to argue with the boy, and so when his call down the hallway went unanswered, he simply sat down and began tucking his napkin into his collar. Ursula put down whatever she was holding on the counter and went by the kitchen table, all the while glaring at Barry. Barry heard her bark out Bruno's name, and the boy came to his seat with his head hung low. Ursula grabbed a warm casserole dish from the stovetop and brought it to the table—some a sort of scalloped potatoes mixture. Barry hated it and he knew Bruno wouldn't touch it. Why Ursula insisted on making things she knew no one would eat was beyond Barry.

"There's red in it." Bruno looked up from his steak. The boy wanted his meat well-done. Most times Barry would accommodate him, but these sirloins had been particularly pricey, and so he was loath to grill them to a blackened crisp.

"Right. That's because I cooked them correctly."

"You know I don't like this. Mum, look, there's blood leaking out of it..."

"It's just the juices, Bruno." Ursula was distracted by cutting into her own steak to determine if Barry had cooked hers medium-well, as she preferred.

Bruno pressed, his voice pitching up into an intolerable whine. "Juice. It's blood! That's wot's inside a cow!" He dropped his cutlery with a clang.

"Quiet." Barry said, but not to Bruno. He'd heard something.

"Can't you, like, microwave this to make it –"

Tap tap

"Shut up, boy!" Barry barked. Ursula jerked her head up to admonish him but stopped when she presumably noticed the tapping.

Metal on glass, Barry thought as he rose from his seat, napkin pulled from his collar already.

He was looking into the living room, but with the next *tap* he realized it was behind him, at the kitchen door. On the other side of the four-paneled window set into the steel door, the barrel of a long pistol was tapping against the glass.

Curiosity overrode fear, and Barry took a step toward the door.

Then he saw the blonde hair shining in the late afternoon sun. The gun barrel shattered the lower right pane of glass. Ursula shrieked once behind him, and a small hand snaked through the broken glass to grasp the deadbolt.

The cleaning girl's hand. He knew because there was a tattoo on the flesh between the thumb and index finger; something that was supposed to be a dove but looked more like a pigeon after being felled by a shotgun blast. And he would recognize his own .357 Magnum *anywhere*.

She'd raided his office to find this address. She'd taken his pistol.

Oh, Christ.

Barry barked out the words he'd never thought he'd have to say. "Into the panic room, now!" he yelled to Ursula and Bruno, who simply stared at him with mouths agape.

"Now!" Barry shouted, pulling Bruno's chair back violently enough to spur them both into action. He stepped out of their way as they ran down the hallway, taking one last look at the kitchen door. The girl had already pulled her hand back in—carefully enough to avoid the broken glass—and was turning the knob, the door coming slowly open...

Barry followed his fleeing family. He was the last one into the panic room and slammed the heavy metal door behind himself. It closed with a semi-satisfying *thunk*.

Ursula was at the far end of the rectangular room, and Barry looked her way. Her face vacillated between fear and anger and something approaching...judgment?

While Barry wrestled with the prospect of trying to explain what was happening, Bruno took the opportunity to press a series of commands into the keypad immediately to the left of the heavy steel door. There was a distinct sequence of four beeps, and then a muffled *clunk* from within the door itself.

Barry's attention turned to his son, whose neck was within wringing distance. "What did you just do, Bruno?" he hissed through clenched teeth.

"That's the lock!" the boy said proudly. "It says right here, *press these numbers to activate the time lock.*"

"Why would you do that?" Barry asked, incredulous.

"So it was locked, Dad."

"Aye, but why would you lock the time lock?"

Bruno hesitated a moment, his face taking on a look that suggested his father hadn't heard him correctly the first time. "So that it was *locked*, Dad."

Barry's hands curled into and out of fists several times. He looked back and forth from Ursula to Bruno. Ursula, for her part, now had a look of unabashed worry on her face.

Bruno wisely backed away from his father until he felt his mother's hand touch his left shoulder. "Should..." he started, "should I not have—"

Barry erupted. "NO, YOU SHOULDN'T HAVE, YOU DAFT 'APETH! WOT THE FOOK IS WRONG WITH YE, LOCKING EVERY FOOKING DOOR THAT CROSSES YER PATH? IT'S LIKE A SICKNESS WITH YA!"

"Barry…" Ursula warned.

"YOU'VE PUT US IN HERE FOR, OH CHRIST…" Barry's eyes now scanned the four different CCTV monitors that had blinked to life as Bruno had punched the code into the keypad. Each showed a countdown from 180 minutes. "THREE HOURS! WE'RE IN HERE FOR THREE FOOKIN' HOURS, YOU—"

"*Barry*," Ursula said more forcefully this time.

"Oh, Christ," Barry repeated and slid down the wall to land on his buttocks.

"Soz, Dad." Bruno had the good sense to also sit on the floor and look at his lap.

Ursula, however, crossed her arms and glared daggers at Barry. She gave him a few minutes to decompress, during which he mostly looked at his hands like he didn't know why they were at the ends of his arms. Her patience wasn't eternal, though.

"Who's the girl, Baz?"

Barry thought of a thousand different lies to tell his wife in the space of ten seconds.

"Baz?" Ursula's tone was one that Barry had rarely heard in all their many years together. "Who is the bird with the gun?"

Barry's head lolled to the side to face Ursula. His eyes focused on her feet. "Wot it is, right, uh, that's our cleaning lady. The office."

"Bobbins," she stared in disbelief.

"Right. At the office, we hired a cleaning girl, uh, lady, to tidy up the place after hours."

"It's a one-person office, Baz. How dirty can it get?"

"Swear down, luv."

"Aye." Ursula murmured, stepping over Barry's outstretched legs, heading toward the CCTV screens near the door.

Barry resumed studying his hands. He wished her tone was more hysterical. This cold, controlled one was terrifying.

Ursula watched the screens for a few moments, saw the girl milling around their kitchen aimlessly. "She's fit."

"Is she?" Barry had the good sense to reply.

"Aye. *Well* fit." Ursula said again in that same chilling tone.

Barry looked up and watched the CCTV monitors over Ursula's

shoulder. The girl seemed to somehow identify the kitchen camera. She skipped over to it, and then something obscured the lens. Barry assumed that the girl had disconnected the camera somehow, but the image resumed, panning around the kitchen. The camera came to a rest on what seemed like the counter beneath its usual corner mounting. He could again see their kitchen table, closer now and at less of a ceiling view.

The girl set what was clearly an oversized purse on the counter nearest the door she'd broken in through. Barry saw her remove an object from the bag and then approach the camera. The girl set something down in front of the lens...a square object that seemed familiar.

A video sprang to life on it, and Barry recognized the setting immediately.

"Oh, it's yer office, Baz..." Ursula said, her tone still cold, some sarcasm edging in.

Barry stood, dreading what might play next.

They both watched the video feed, a coldness creeping up Barry's spine. On it, he called out silently – as there was no audio in the home's CCTV setup – to someone while seated at his cluttered desk. He identified the gift frame on the right side of his desk, exactly where he told Ursula he'd placed it. Barry almost blurted out *I told you so* to Ursula, but then thought better of it.

On the video, the girl stuck her head tentatively into Barry's office, clearly responding to his voice. Some sort of dialogue ensued between them; Barry was often laughing, the girl slowly inching into the room as if drawn by his words. At last, the girl walked further into Barry's office, out of the view of the office security camera. On the video, Barry started undoing his belt.

In the silence of the panic room, Barry put his hand to his forehead and winced.

"Oh, look, Baz, you're getting your kecks off for her."

"Lulu, don't watch—"

"Shut it!" she spat toward him, her brow creased in absolute rage, then she turned back to the screen.

The girl came back into the frame.

"Oh, look, Baz, she's got her tits out."

Across the room, Bruno's head perked up. Barry lowered his in shame.

On the video feed, the girl wedged herself between Barry's bulk and his desk. She dropped to her knees. Barry reached toward the gift frame and turned it face down on the desk.

Ursula looked away from the CCTV monitor, then crossed the room to stand next to her seated son.

Barry could see the rest of the coupling play out on the tiny screen. He didn't need to watch it further to know how short the video would be. He now understood that the girl had somehow gotten her hands on the office security camera's memory card, taken it home and transferred the video file to a USB stick, and then plugged *that* into the purloined anniversary frame. And taken the massive .357 Magnum out of his desk for good measure.

What he didn't know was why.

The frame was taken away from the kitchen camera, restoring the view of the counter, the table, the girl. As Barry watched, perplexed, she sat down in his seat and started carving into his steak. She took a bite, then made an exaggerated face of disgust and tossed the silverware to the table. Barry could hear nothing through the massive steel door; the kitchen might as well have been on the moon for all it mattered.

Next, the girl placed herself in Ursula's chair and similarly carved a piece of steak. After tasting it, she looked at the camera and once again made a face, letting the half-chewed piece of meat roll off her tongue to fall to the floor. Just when Barry expected her to do the same with Bruno's meal, he saw that she remained seated in Bruno's chair, elbows moving frantically as she cut up the steak and ate it. To Barry's shock, she stood after a few minutes of this and displayed Bruno's plate, completely devoid of food. Bruno's entire dinner had been eaten.

First time that's happened, Barry mused.

From across the room, Ursula spoke icily. "Wot's this slag's name, Baz?"

Barry nearly jumped at the broken silence. "Uhm, it's..." Barry struggled to remember.

"You always did have a soft spot for blondes." Ursula rolled her eyes and crossed her arms tightly across her chest. "Never mind. Wot's Goldilocks doing now?"

"She's, uhm..." Barry no longer saw the girl in the kitchen's video feed.

He squinted at the four monitors until he managed to identify the girl stretched out in his recliner, in the living room. Barry's massive pistol rested in her lap, and the girl had her hands behind her head in a perfect pose of comfort.

"Uh, living room, on my chair..."

Goldilocks sprang up from the recliner, posted her fists on her hips in mock disappointment, then leveled the pistol and pulled the trigger. The bullet blew a massive hole in the back of Barry's favorite chair, a slightly smaller one in the wall behind it, and then came to a rest somewhere near the home's foundation.

All three of them jumped at the roar of the gun. The steel container muffled most of the sound, but not all of it. Ursula regained her composure and was staring daggers again at Barry, who wore a sheepish look but stayed quiet. Barry saw that Bruno was looking back and forth between his parents, probably wondering why they weren't putting a stop to this girl's antics. Bruno, too, had the good sense to remain silent.

In the interim, Goldilocks had moved on to the master bedroom and seated herself at Ursula's vanity. The girl had a finger in her ear, rubbing vigorously, obviously trying in vain to restore some hearing. Her mouth made various shapes.

"She's at your vanity," Barry reported, immediately regretting his decision.

Ursula stormed over, her voice rising as she came. "Whore's gonna cadge our makeup!"

They watched Goldilocks entertain herself in the mirror for a few moments. Then she stood and, holding the pistol in her right hand, gripped the right edge of Ursula's vanity with her left hand and violently overturned it. Every bit of perfume and makeup went to the floor. The mirror showed a chain of massive cracks. Goldilocks turned to the camera fastened in an upper corner of the room and performed an exaggerated shrug to it, then went out of the room.

Ursula looked at Barry, mere inches from his face. "She's peckin' me 'ead, Baz. You stick your mingin' tool past her Newtons, and here we are with a wrecked gaff."

"Lulu, I'll get the vanity fettled," Barry offered meekly.

"Fook the fooking vanity, Baz! This is about yer inability to keep yer pecker in yer duds. *Consequences*, Baz."

Barry's sphincter practically inverted.

Unnoticed by either of them, Bruno had waddled over. His stomach growled loud enough for them both to turn and look down at him.

"My tummy thinks my throat's cut," Bruno whinged.

Both parents were about to shout "shut it!" in unison, but motion on a CCTV screen caught their attention.

"Hey! That girl's in our room! She's...she's touching our computer! MA!" Bruno yelled.

Before either could address this, Goldilocks put her feet up on Bruno's keyboard hard enough to send plastic keys spraying up from the device. She gave a dramatic yawn-and-stretch gesture while pushing back which resulted in her falling backward in Bruno's coveted gaming chair. Mid-fall, Goldilocks' finger closed on the trigger of the pistol—still in her right hand—and Bruno's laptop was reduced to a smoking ruin. All three in the panic room jumped once again.

Bruno wailed loudly enough for both Barry and Ursula to clamp their hands on their ears. In Bruno's room, Goldilocks stood and, leaving Bruno's expensive chair in two parts on the floor, skipped merrily back to the master bedroom.

Less angry and more alarmed now, Ursula took the whimpering Bruno by the elbow and led him back toward the other end of the panic room. They sat cross-legged on the ground and spoke to each other in soft tones. Barry looked away from them and back to the CCTV monitors. The timer at the bottom of each screen showed 120 minutes. This was nowhere near over.

Goldilocks sequestered herself in the master suite and slowly disrobed, doing a seductive dance to the camera. Bruno said a silent prayer of thanks that he was the only one able to see this display, then sent an equally silent curse crotch-ward as his manhood began to perk up. The girl seemed to tire of her own performance and laid down on the bed. There she remained for the next hour, sleeping face down, naked as the day she was born, splayed across the entire queen-sized bed.

WITH THE TIMER on the CCTV screens counting down with agonizing slowness from 60 minutes, Barry noticed movement again on the screen showing his bed. He had been staring into the middle distance for the better part of the last hour, not daring to glance over at his wrathful wife or his inconsolable son. He looked up and noticed Goldilocks was gone from his bed.

The hallway camera feed showed a shapely, naked arse moving across its face. The kitchen camera, its angle reduced considerably by being taken off the ceiling and put on the counter, showed the girl moving toward her large purse with a sluggish gait. She rummaged in it, her arms sunk practically to the elbows in its depths, then came out with several objects that Barry couldn't identify. No, wait, four objects, and he could identify two of them: a small cigarette lighter and a belt. Goldilocks was now opening and slamming shut various kitchen drawers. Barry watched in confusion as she opened the final drawer and withdrew a spoon. Then his view was of her fully nude front as she walked with renewed purpose back to the hallway.

Barry expected to see her return to his bedroom, but instead she veered into Bruno's and flopped onto his small twin bed, her long hair bouncing before coming to a rest across her shoulders. Goldilocks rose to a seated position on Bruno's bed, her legs crossed, her brow knitted in concentration, and she fiddled with one of the objects she'd gotten from her purse.

"Oh, this is well bad." Barry's hand rose to his mouth and covered it absently.

Ursula had raised her head upon hearing him speak; he saw this in his peripheral vision. She slowly rose and trundled over to him. "Wot's yer bessie doing n—"

Barry quieted her by extending his left arm and guiding Ursula down to a seated position next to him.

They both watched the screen in rapt horror as Goldilocks shut off the lighter that had been positioned under the purloined spoon. She picked up the syringe and sucked the contents of the spoon into it, then held the syringe absently in her mouth while she affixed the belt to her right thigh.

Bruno started to stand. "Wot's she doing n—"

Both of them turned to him, their eyes wide, and cried "Stay there!" To Bruno's credit, he sank back down to the floor and pouted.

Upon turning back to the CCTV monitors, Ursula and Barry saw that Goldilocks had already injected herself. She pulled the needle out from between the first and second toes on her right foot, dropped the forgotten syringe on Bruno's bedspread, loosened the belt tourniquet on her thigh, and slowly lowered herself onto the bed. They saw her eyes, already half-lidded, close and her right hand meander toward her naked crotch.

Ursula stood, her anger back in full force, glaring down at the top of Barry's balding head. She reared back with her right foot and gave him a forceful kick to the bottom of his left thigh. Barry said "Ow," but didn't react otherwise, his eyes glued to the CCTV screen.

"Fooking pig," Ursula swore, turning to march back to the far end of the panic room.

"Oh, no. No, no no no no...please no." Barry droned, his voice rising with each uttered denial.

Ursula turned and had her mouth set wide, her left index finger already poised to thrust in his direction, but stopped when she saw Barry turn absolutely white. She jogged back over awkwardly and viewed the screen with him.

On it, Goldilocks' nude body was practically dancing on top of Bruno's Minecraft bed set. Her legs and arms were straight, rigid even, and her head thrashed to the left and right.

"She's having a fit," Ursula observed coolly.

"She's overdosing." Barry managed, his voice strangled and high-pitched.

Even as they watched, Goldilocks' seizure rattled to a close, her body changed from nearly vibrating to simply jerking, then to a deathly repose punctuated by a few remaining twitches that caused Barry and Ursula to gasp each time.

Then Goldilocks was still; her chest was no longer rising and falling. Finally, to their horror, Barry and Ursula saw a dark liquid issue from between her legs, bubble, and then seep into Bruno's bedspread.

Ursula did the sign of the cross and lowered her head. Barry couldn't tear his eyes away from the screen. Neither of them noticed that Bruno had crept over until he exclaimed "Naked bird on our bed!"

Barry turned and guided both of them back to the far end of the panic room, then returned to the CCTV screens to watch the remaining minutes count down. He sighed and once again slid down the wall to land heavily on his arse.

Barry thought of the coming conversations to be had: with the police; with his son; with Lulu. He did not look forward to any of them. It seemed that every time he had to talk to someone, it was always to his detriment. It had been like that for years. It wasn't likely to change.

THE IMMORTAL DAN
SINCLAIR

This isn't my first trip to Idaho, but it's certainly been my most painful. I guess I should add "so far" to that statement. My situation often makes me regret stating anything as an absolute.

Hi. My name is Dan Sinclair. And I'm immortal.

Not to split hairs here, but I want to make sure everyone understands the difference between "immortal" and "invincible." *Immortal* means that I can't die. Or, more to the point in my particular case, when I *do* actually die, I'm immediately revived. *Invincible* would mean I'm too powerful to be overcome or defeated, effectively impervious to harm or death.

Oh, boy, I am here to tell you...that ain't the case.

Anyways, about Idaho. Most wild wolf packs in Idaho are in the center of the state, and so I went to what I determined to be the center – near Chamberlain Basin. Which is, by the way, directly south of Elk City. Since wolves there primarily hunt elk, you would think they'd be closer to Elk City. Because, y'know, it's in the name. There's got to be tons of elk there.

Get it?

Never mind.

I got to Chamberlain Basin and went about finding some wolves to attack me. This wasn't as easy as one might think. First off, most wolves are terrified of humans, even lone humans. And I don't blame them, either. The average human is just the worst, honestly. Just downright assholes, a vast majority of us. So I get it. Wolves aren't going to be, like, *Oh, look, dude, that stupid human is out trudging through the snow alone. Let's go get his liver.* Personally, I think it's more like *Uh-oh, my canines, we should bail. It's a human. Maybe even an American one. There's a huge chance he has a gun. Cheese it!*

The point is that it was hard to get attacked by a pack of wolves.

I won't bore anyone with *how* I managed to get attacked by a pack of wolves. Just rest assured that I have. And man, does it fucking *hurt*.

So, picture it: I'm lying here in a puddle of my own sweat, piss, blood, and myriad other bodily substances. My parka is in tatters. Likewise my flannel shirt, and the shirt under that, and my pants, even my boots, and so on and so forth. I'm shivering like mad because, well, *shock*...and it's like 28 degrees. That's Fahrenheit, mind you, because *America*.

What I assume to be the Alpha has his snout buried in my lower torso. He dips his head so far in there that his eyes disappear quite often. Just a couple of twitchy, flat-lying ears in view most of the time. And of course when he does pull out of me, he's looking right into my face. He's not used to things making eye contact with him and screaming or, by now, just grunting really, while he's feasting on their innards. The other wolves have formed a perimeter around me. I think this is less in deference to the commotion I'm making and more about respect for the Alpha, but maybe it's a combination of both. Hell if I know.

Impossible to describe the pain of a wolf rooting around in your innards. As I mentioned, I'm not any more or less impervious to anything than you are; I just get to live through whatever horrible death is lined up for me (or in this case, I arranged), and feel the pain of the whole thing the whole time. Granted, just like regular, non-immortal folks like you, Nature has a way of blunting pain. Shock. Nerve damage. The brain shutting down, et cetera. There's been tons of studies on it. I'll be goddamned if any of those studies are going to be done on *me*, mind you, but we'll get to that. Just know that while it's pretty much the most painful thing you can possibly imagine, it's still blunted a bit by Nature.

Hey, *thanks,* Nature!

My biggest fear during this whole "being eaten by a pack of wolves" event is that they won't finish the job. Given my...condition...I only really die – and therefore reset – if my brain is completely destroyed. I have no control over what part of me they eat. I had originally considered breaching my own skull in order to entice them, but that would've rendered me pretty much unconscious or at least dumber than usual, so I chose not to. And I need my wits about me to make sure I don't spend the better part of the winter here as a hollowed out – but fully aware and alive – husk. Or worse, get happened upon by some idiot hiker or park ranger with a hard-on for a hero badge who would save me. And by save me, I mean bring me before doctors and/or scientists in my most vulnerable state. That, my friends, would be the worst-case scenario.

Things look to be going my way, however. While the Alpha is merely nose deep in my entrails – is that my spleen hanging out of his mouth? – several others from the pack have moved in and are nipping at me. When the Alpha doesn't rebuke them, it's *game on.* One particularly gorgeous animal bites down hard on my genitals and pulls them away from my body like they were only scotch-taped there. Another goes after my feet; the tickling sensation is actually worse than the pain for a moment. Yet another one helps itself to my eyes. I mean, most of my face too, but my eyes are all I care about. I can't monitor the situation very well without my eyes.

In the darkness, I lose track of time. By now I don't feel pain any longer, just pressure and pushing/pulling. Much like when you go to the dentist and get a mouth full of Novocain; you know he's in there doing horrendous things to your teeth – your body – but because you can't feel the pain, you allow it. Most of us live our lives that way; so long as the pain is numbed, we're okay with all manner of horrible shit happening to us. I'll take this respite from my senses to describe a bit about what's to come after the *coup de grace*, which I hope is coming soon.

Now, you might be expecting me to illustrate what it's like to be dead, or to describe moving through space and time as an untethered soul, privy to all sorts of cosmic secrets; that I would come face to face with God or the Devil or whomever you imagine is running shit and really give them what for. That, at the very least, I can provide some sort of insight into the nature of our species, the universe, the soul.

Well, welcome to Disappointmentville. Population: you.

I wake up with a jolt...not just in my brain, but my entire body. Like every cell reached over and touched the electric fence. It's more than a physical sensation, it's...everything, everywhere. Sorry, I don't mean to get so esoteric. It's just...*boom*.

I always wake up in Vermont. No, I'm not going to tell you where. Suffice to say that after I woke up in the same place a dozen or so times, I built myself a house there. So now I appear naked and fully formed in my own house rather than whatever else might've been built here otherwise: a parking lot. A ranger station. A Hooters. I don't know. This all started in the early 1800s. Fortunately, there weren't a lot of people milling about whenever I materialized there, y'know, before the house got built.

I won't bother telling you much about my childhood – both for my own safety and for your mental health. I'm an orphan who never knew his parents, and who came up through the "system," such as it was back then. Basically, I was an indentured farmhand for most of my childhood and teen years, but it beat living on the street. I kept to myself, was strong enough not to be preyed on by the bigger kids – most of the time – and took advantage of my natural intelligence to constantly improve my station. Whether my parents gave me up, died of tuberculosis, or never existed is academic; at no point did I have parents. It's that simple.

The first time I died was pretty miserable. It was late 1832 and cholera had landed in New York. *Ever heard of plumbing, Europe? Miserable bastards.* Fortunately, I was not autopsied. Also fortunately, I was pitched into a furnace in a hastily arranged cremation. And by "fortunately," I mean I got to experience being burned "alive" for the first time – but definitely not the last. However, the good thing about this was – you guessed it – my brain tissue got destroyed in short order. The next thing I knew I was naked and afraid in Vermont way before reality T.V. was invented.

You can imagine my confusion. Or maybe you can't, I don't know. I really have no way of knowing how creative your brain is. Trust me, it was confusing. I wish I could say that I resurrected as a clean slate, or maybe even coming back as a baby would've been better; a blissfully ignorant, wailing infant, shitting himself amongst the pine trees. But no, I awoke still thinking I was on fire, shouting and flailing about, remembering everything.

Blah blah stealing clothes from clothes lines. Blah blah resuming my previous identity and telling everyone it was a clerical mistake. I wasn't close to anyone, so this last part wasn't that big of a deal. I don't need to describe what I did to survive, I simply took what I needed so long as I wasn't hurting anyone else. Almost nobody noticed me. If you think people are self-centered in this century, you should've seen them in the nineteenth. You could die from a toothache back then. Most people were either all-in on making sure they survived, or fully committed to dying as quickly as possible via drinking or drugs. Either way, they weren't paying attention to my skinny ass.

Along with *fucking cholera*, the early 1830s gave us the proliferation of the public library system. This ended up being the event that shaped my life more than any other. If I wasn't sitting all day in a library reading, then I was traveling between them or I was working in one. I relied on the kindness of strangers quite often, mostly for food, but of course held them at arm's length. It wouldn't do any good for people to get to know me, find out I died somehow, and then see me show up again. Trust me, there's only so many times you can pull that trick before people call bullshit.

The other thing I figured out after my first death was that it appar-

ently arrested my physical development. Up until that point, I was growing, getting older, etcetera. When I died in 1832 at the ripe old age of
twenty-four (I think. I'm guessing), I never got any older than twenty-
four. This compounded my need to stay out of meaningful relationships
and also caused me to need to travel. Once I ran out of libraries to work at,
I pivoted to a living as a traveling book salesman. Sometimes it was the
Bible (by death number eight I no longer believed a syllable of it), sometimes it was the dictionary, and eventually it was encyclopedias. Setting up
a company with a mysterious, reclusive owner (Mr. D. Sinclair) and oper-
ating as an independent contractor served my needs nicely.

In short, I got by. I scraped up enough money to make some invest-
ments and, with the help of a savvy accountant who possibly realized yet
didn't care that Mr. D. Sinclair's son and heir looked and sounded exactly
like Mr. D. Sinclair himself, managed to become a man of leisure. This
was about 1940. So don't look at me like I'm the one percent. I worked
my ass off longer than both of your parents combined, pal.

To my shame, I managed to avoid both World War One *and* World
War Two. In my defense, if I had been wounded over there and lost
control of my body, or "killed" and shipped home in a box and interred in
a box and...well, you get the idea...it would've caused a lot more problems
than draft-dodging did. By the time Korea and Vietnam happened, I had
avoided dying long enough to be ineligible for the draft by virtue of my
"age" on paper.

Yes, I'm aware I've skipped directly from the early nineteenth century
to the middle of the twentieth. I can sum up the years I've glossed over
thusly: influenza, typhus, consumption, influenza, influenza, smallpox,
run over by horse and carriage, measles, influenza (technically suicide by
pistol that time), syphilis, fire, polio (again a pistol), drowned (and fortunately eaten by sharks and other fish), and pneumonia.

I learned to carry my *last will and testament* on my person at all times.
It explicitly and repeatedly stipulated that no matter how I died, my body
was to be cremated and my ashes saved for my young heir, who would be
along to collect them shortly. You should've seen my collection of urns in
1920. But I couldn't trust the U.S. military not to override my wishes.
Wolves covered in my blood to the contrary, I'm pretty risk averse.

Oh, and before you ask, no, I don't have a weak immune system.

None of you fuckers would've survived in those times either. Go ask your grandmother how *her* grandmother died if you don't believe me.

I wish that I could regale you with tales of my conquests of women (and occasionally men), but at the end of the day, all of them are either gone or no longer in my life. In the 1980s, I died of AIDS once (ask me why I'm pro-LGBTQ. Go ahead). I've had to harden my heart so often that it's little more than a throbbing callus at this point. I've borne no children that I'm aware of; I'm terrified of dooming someone else to my unique fate.

And of course, I've no doubt that someone out there is saying that I'm an ungrateful wretch for not sharing the gift of immortality that God has given me. That there must be some higher purpose for me. That I'm selfish for not giving myself over to science for the betterment of the species. That there must be *a reason*.

Listen to me very carefully: Most of you are so bad at living life that giving you *one* chance at it is a fucking joke, let alone multiple chances. Most of you can't deal with minor inconveniences, which COVID-19 proved pretty eloquently, by the way, let alone major ones. None of you have any pain tolerance whatsoever, neither physical nor emotional. Of course there are exceptions like Mother Teresa or Einstein out there. But give them immortality and you just might get to see their ugly sides, and by then it would be too late to reverse the decision. In my opinion, you should be grateful that the only immortal that I know of – me – keeps to himself and does no harm to others as a rule. I have to be the lesser of many, many evils. That's the only thing that keeps me going at all.

Sorry. Bitterness tends to creep into everything over time.

You might also be wondering why I'm giving this confession. Well, for one thing, any identifying details have been lies. Don't bother looking for me in Vermont. And my name isn't the name I provided. I live in the internet age too, you know. I'm not stupid.

At long last, you might be curious as to why I've pitched myself into the waiting mouths of this flawless pack of wolves in good ole' Idaho. The answer is nothing less than the scourge of our time: cancer. Non-Hodgkin's Lymphoma, to be exact. And the reason I've chosen the wolves is actually relatively simple: One or two times, I've resurrected with the same maladies that I died with. Cirrhosis. Crohn's disease. Chlamydia.

And so I'm not taking any chances; I'm aiming for the complete and unique obliteration of every individual organ. I wish I could've trusted Western medicine with this, because it would've been considerably less painful. But no, that's not likely to happen in my lifetime...pun intended.

I don't feel the Idaho cold on my skin. Honestly, I'm not sure if I felt it after that first pure, vicious bite to my naked abdomen by the Alpha wolf a few minutes ago. I knew I could count on these magnificent animals in the end.

Finally, one of those big, beautiful, furry bastards chomps down hard enough on my skull to fracture it, and it's as if they've never smelled anything so amazing in their lives as my brain. It's possible I've ruined some of these wolves for elk or reindeer or rabbit or who knows what forever. I know that more than one of them is taking a run at my squishy gray matter because I can feel their swollen tongues touching it from different angles. It gets progressively harder to think. At long last, one of the wolves destroys the center of my consciousness and it's like being switched off.

Boom.

Wish me luck.

K'cetnoc & the Eternal Journey, Part 3: Kevin, Part 2

"Dude, when Britt said you were, like, all rocks and shit...I thought she just meant that you were, like, dumb," Kevin shouted over the music.

K'cetnoc leaned gingerly against the bar. Below his considerable bulk were two ruined iron barstools that had failed to hold his weight. Both he and Kevin were glowering at Brittani DiMarco, who danced within an ever-increasing circle of men alongside her friend Cyndi.

"But you're not! You're actually a cool dude, dude." Kevin again raised his voice, unsure if K'cetnoc's lack of response was based on the volume of the throbbing bass, his attention being focused on their mutual unrequited crush on the distant dance floor, or his disdain of Kevin.

Finally, K'cetnoc turned and looked at Kevin. What passed for a forlorn look etched his already stony features. "K'CETNOC IS PLEAS-ANTLY SURPRISED TO FIND KEVIN'S COMPANY BEARABLE AS WELL. KEVIN IS MUCH LESS THE 'WALKING DILDO' THAT BRITTANI CHARACTERIZED KEVIN AS."

"Thanks, bro. Wait, what?" Kevin blinked as he registered the massive, rocky being's words.

They were interrupted by a thin, twitchy woman who, at first, tapped on K'cetnoc's massive shoulder, then resorted to pounding it with her fist to gain his attention. "Satmeth?"

K'cetnoc, his mood sour and growing sourer with each young man who inched closer to Brittani, gleefully thrusting their crotches near her posterior, ignored the woman.

The woman, whose face was covered in acne scars, turned to Kevin and spoke into his ear. Kevin recoiled, either from the volume of her voice or the smell of her breath.

"Dude, 'Cet!" Kevin called. "Yo, this Betty wants some of the tweak on your arm, bro!" Kevin found this terribly amusing for reasons that escaped the ancient lapidarian colossus.

For her part, the girl sidled back over to K'cetnoc, holding open the top of her dingy halter top to provide him with a full view of her tiny breasts. "I'll blow ya for it, big guy." She smiled up at K'cetnoc, who wasn't sure if he'd ever seen teeth that color on a human.

"THERE ARE NOT ANY ILLEGAL SUBSTANCES ON K'CETNOC'S PERSON."

He turned from the pouting meth head and refocused his gaze on Brittani. She had now drifted away from Cyndi and had her arms around the neck of a man who was brazenly running his hands up and down her sides as they danced.

"Dude, this is some bullshit," Kevin remarked to no one in particular. He motioned to the bartender and ordered four shots of tequila. "Here, man, have some Patrizzle."

K'cetnoc looked down despairingly at the proffered shot glasses. Despite already having explained to Kevin that his constitution prevented him from experiencing the effects of alcohol, the young man had been purchasing drinks for the Keeper of Planets and Warden of Sol all night. K'cetnoc had existed before the creation of every body in this solar system save its sun, but his patience was nearly exhausted. He carefully gripped the tiny glass, lifted it, and tossed back the thick, clear liquid.

"Yeah, bro!" Kevin followed suit, elated at the idea of no longer drinking alone.

K'cetnoc drank the other shot. Brittani had told both K'cetnoc and Kevin that they "should" come out to the club "tonight" because "why not?" Both had considered that they were still being led on by the young, chestnut-maned beauty; both still showed up hoping for some of her attention.

Thus far, that had not happened. Brittani had waved in their general direction once nearly an hour ago. Neither Kevin nor K'cetnoc knew which of them the gesture was meant for, and so their moods had mutually curdled. They had both waved back, though.

The combination of the chaotic dance floor, the pounding pop music, the throng of people three deep at the bar, and the second approach of the meth-addled woman all conspired to bring about an even darker feeling in K'cetnoc. While Kevin seemed to be managing his despair with copious amounts of alcohol, K'cetnoc could experience no such escape. He hadn't been this miserable since his lover Artamon Matveyev had abandoned their affair in favor of assisting a young, so-called "Peter the Great" with running Russia. K'cetnoc mused that nearly half the people in this nightclub probably had a similar tale of woe, and that he was not special.

The meth woman slid a scaly hand across K'cetnoc's thigh, searching fruitlessly for his crotch. "Come on, man," she whined, then looked up in a manner that approximated seduction.

"AS K'CETNOC TOLD YOU, K'CETNOC DOESN'T HAVE..." K'cetnoc's patience finally snapped. "YOU KNOW WHAT. SURE. THIS IS BENITOITE. IT IS EXCLUSIVELY FROM CALIFORNIA."

The woman cooed as K'cetnoc broke a shard of the blue crystal from his right forearm.

"THIS IS AN EXTREMELY RARE SUBSTANCE, OCCURRING IN ONLY A SINGLE VALLEY IN A SINGLE AREA OF YOUR PLANET. IT SELLS FOR NEARLY FOUR THOUSAND DOLLARS A CARAT."

The woman's eyes began watering, mistaking the mineral for actual methamphetamine.

K'cetnoc placed the crystal shard on the bar and brought his fist down firmly on it. When he took his craggy paw away, there was only blue powder where the rock had been. "K'CETNOC BELIEVES THE SAYING IS 'KNOCK YOURSELF OUT.'"

Without another word, and with all pretense at sexual favor abandoned, the woman deftly swept the powder into her palm and bolted for the nearby door. Once she was outside, K'cetnoc saw her huddle with two friends, both of whom hazarded furtive glances back into the club at the massive lithoid being.

"Dude, solid." Kevin's head nodded, his eyes half-lidded. At some point he had procured several more shot glasses filled with the syrup he called "tequila." He pushed one in K'cetnoc's direction with two wavering fingers.

K'cetnoc fixed his gaze on the dance floor. Brittani and the man she danced with were standing nearly stock still, their mouths locked together in a deep kiss. They were oblivious to both the dancing around them and the people who stopped to stare at their very public display of affection. K'cetnoc wasn't sure how much time passed, but as he watched, the man very patiently worked his hands south to the hem of Brittani's miniskirt. Soon, those same hands disappeared under it.

In his peripheral vision, K'cetnoc saw a panicked man fight his way to the bar and heard him ask the bartender to call "nine-one-one," as there were "a couple of chicks" in the parking lot with "fucking blood just shooting out their noses."

Kevin was now moving his head back and forth approximately in time with the music, his nose about two inches from the bar top. He held an unlit cigarette in the fingers of his left hand and a lighter curled in his right.

K'cetnoc refocused on the dance floor but could not locate Brittani and her young suitor. He pushed himself away from the bar, which elicited a concerned look from one of the bartenders who had apparently not realized K'cetnoc was real. K'cetnoc carefully knifed through the crowd, searching for any sign of Brittani.

K'cetnoc found none.

After a full circuit of the club, K'cetnoc's view fell back upon Kevin and the open door behind him. Kevin's head was fully pressed into the bar, and behind his profile, K'cetnoc could see red and blue emergency lights flashing. He turned away and looked upwards in frustration. Were he to shed the matter that comprised this iteration of his body in the club, he might injure several patrons. It was not their fault that K'cetnoc could not pick a healthy relationship to save his life. Also, since he was nearly immortal and would persist until the heat death of the universe, or at least until Sol swelled to a red giant and then shrank into a white dwarf, the metaphor was moot. But then he saw her.

About thirty feet away, sequestered in a corner of the night club's ceiling, a gorgeous arachnid sat placidly in her web, staring at him. When she saw him return her gaze, she turned slightly and busied herself with maintaining the silky strands which threatened to shake loose from their moorings with every thump of bass. But then she turned back and locked her many eyes on him.

K'cetnoc had never seen a more beautiful being in his entire existence and was instantly smitten. *"PHYLLONETA IMPRESSA,"* he called to the spider using her scientific name, unsure if his voice would carry to the hairs she used for hearing.

After a pause during which K'cetnoc's heart hitched in his rocky chest, the spider opened her chelicera at him, and he knew that the attraction was mutual.

The Necromancer of Parga

One of the best things about the end of the world was the steady stream of men willing to work merely for food. The other was the never-ending supply of bodies.

Athanasios Hasapis watched the caravan wind its way up the ancient stone stairs of Parga Castle. His view from the top was clear for three-hundred-and-sixty degrees; three sides faced the sea, one the Greek town of Parga. From the sixteenth century until now, in the late twenty-first, it remained impossible to sneak up on this hilltop citadel. He was confident there would be no twenty-second century, and so for all intents and purposes, it would remain secure for eternity. He repaired to a nearby lounge chair in the open vestibule, grateful for the shade.

Athos – as he thought of himself but allowed no one to address him – motioned subtly with his right hand to one of the Tonys. The man strode to him and lowered his head to receive Athos' order.

"There are several men coming up bearing a good deal of cargo. They should be disarmed before entering my presence."

Tony straightened and nodded in a precise motion, then turned and went past the other Tony to intercept the incoming entourage. The remaining Tony kept his guard at the left side of the open archway, but he moved ever so slightly to the right to compensate for the lack of his comrade.

Athos referred to both of his bodyguards as Tony; they were interchangeable and indiscernible from each other. He had no idea what their actual names were. They were Italian, and so they were Tony. They were the only people he allowed within a two-meter radius of himself at any given time.

Athos expected there to be quite an argument between the men coming up and the descending Tony. Most of the men approaching were what the past world would have considered "spies" and "elite soldiers." Like those of America's famous Central Intelligence Agency, SEAL teams, and Special Forces, except from its European counterparts. All of them would be loath to relinquish their weapons; these were the sort of men who slept with their hands curled around pistols well before society had disintegrated.

He'd dispatched the main team, made up of mostly former Albanian *SHISH* agents, to Geneva to obtain the bulk of the materials, which were now snaking their way castle-ward in massive wooden boxes. The second, smaller team was a mixture of former Greek *EYP* and Serbian *BIA* operatives. Their mission involved obtaining various chemicals and medical supplies from anywhere they could get them. Athos didn't feel the need to micromanage team two the way he did team one. Any idiots could perform team two's tasks. Team three was made up exclusively of former Turkish *MIT* agents, and their mission had been simple but perilous-- procure heroin. Again, Athos didn't care how, so long as they weren't traced back to Greece.

Teams two and three had returned to Castle Parga within five and seven days of dispatch, respectively. Athos had secured their booty in the confines of his lab several stories below and dismissed their personnel. The stone battlements were getting crowded.

Team one had been dispatched three weeks ago, by Athos' count. He understood that making their way back from Switzerland to Greece was roughly an eight-day journey by foot – more if you avoided Italy completely – and so their return was relatively prompt. They could have teleported to Geneva for all he cared, but coming back with their precious cargo must have been perilous. He made a mental note to question the team's lead for the details.

Athos heard the sort of commotion which heralds the arrival of a dozen sweaty, tired men. He saw Tony tense and widen his stance in the archway. The bodyguard moved with fluid grace to allow the other Tony through, then blocked the entryway again.

Athos waited until the first Tony stood before him. One single bead of sweat on his forehead betrayed the past minutes spent in the unforgiving Grecian sun, haggling with the brutes over whether their knives constituted weapons or not. Tony waited patiently for Athos to acknowledge him. Athos raised his right eyebrow.

"Sir, they are disarmed, and distinctly unhappy about it."

Athos nodded as if this were the most obvious thing that could have been said.

"Sir, there are four containers outside, should I have them brought in?"

Athos favored Tony with a rare grin. "Thank you, Tony, well done. Yes, please have them brought down to my lab. And I would like the team leader to accompany them. I will leave it to you and Tony to decide who guards the rest and who will remain with me."

Tony's response was again a curt nod. He turned on his heel smartly and went back out through the archway, into the heat.

Athos turned away from the light flooding in through the open archways and made his way down a slim, stone stairwell for several flights. He arrived at one of the many "secret" doors to his laboratory, such as it was in this primitive stronghold, and punched the entry code into the keypad.

The air conditioning was a welcome relief. Athos remained hidden behind a large bank of machinery, his view of the men depositing the long wooden boxes interrupted by the monolithic structures of mainframe computers and other electronics. He waited until the eight men who had borne the cargo reluctantly turned and left the coolness of the lab before approaching. Tony stood to the right of the boxes with the team leader next to him. The man looked nervous. Athos tried to recall his name but could not.

Tony spoke up with preternatural helpfulness. "Sir, this is Mirjet, team one's leader."

Athos flashed a smile at Tony so quickly he doubted that Mirjet even caught it. The man was looking at the myriad cables snaking across the ceiling like a tourist seeing a skyscraper for the first time. Athos seated himself and crossed his legs at the knee.

When Athos spoke, Mirjet snapped to attention. "Did you encounter any resistance in Geneva, Mirjet?" Athos regarded the man's dark, tanned skin and ubiquitous black mustache.

Mirjet attempted to speak, realized his throat was completely dry, swallowed, and then tried again. "Sir. We had no problem getting into the country, but there were pockets of resistance in Geneva itself. However, once we dispatched those, we found very little around the WHO office itself."

Athos nearly winced at Mirjet's pronunciation of the World Health Organization's acronym as the word *who* rather than *double-you aitch oh*, but he remained stoic. He couldn't imagine what the Albanian thought upon meeting him in person; the initial mission details had been provided to Mirjet by the other Tony. Mirjet was built like a footballer, broad at the shoulders and hips but without a hint of fat. He was less than two meters tall. He reminded Athos of an Iranian wrestler whose name escaped him...

By contrast, Athos stood over two meters tall and was thin. His former countrymen in the United States would have called him "lanky." He was coming up on sixty-years of age, and his hair had gone both long and gray in the past years of pandemic, panic, and societal collapse. His face was severe, his eyes small but piercing, his nose thin, his mouth cruel. Athos appreciated these aspects of his appearance—all the better to control weak-minded men with.

"Were there any left alive at the *double-you aitch oh*?"

"No, sir, not a one. But we did as you ordered and brought you the freshest ones we could, given your...parameters." Mirjet's voice trailed off, his eyes scanning the middle distance in remembrance of the carnage he'd seen in Geneva and all points between there and here.

"And you weren't pursued? Followed by anyone, in any way?" Athos raised his eyebrows in question.

"No, sir, we were not. Absolutely positive."

After a very long, very uncomfortable pause – for Mirjet, at least –

Athos clapped his hands on his thighs and rose. "Well, let's see what we have, then."

Without having to be told, Tony directed Mirjet to the head of the first wooden box and, taking up the opposite end, guided the box to a medical berth at the far end of the laboratory. They lifted the box on top of an ambulance gurney situated perpendicular to a hospital bed replete with clean, white sheets. Mirjet eyed the bed as if he hadn't seen either sheets or a bed in months.

Tony and Mirjet repeated the operation three more times. Tony then gently placed his hand on Mirjet's elbow and guided him away from the four medical stations. They remained at attention a good two meters from both the stations and Athos.

"Tony, please show Mirjet and his men to the barracks. They may enjoy all unsecured areas of the castle, but they must not leave the grounds." Athos moved his eyes from Tony and fixed them on Mirjet "Under pain of death."

Mirjet whitened a little but had the sense to give a grateful nod to Athos. Tony guided him out of the laboratory, then followed.

Alone again, at last. Athos could already smell the death. He took a deep inhalation through his nose, then wedged a small crowbar into the lid of the first box.

Athanasios Hasapis was born on the island of Crete, on the American Air Force/Naval base there, to an American mother and Greek father. His father had been an aviation mechanic fortunate enough to be trained by the Americans, while his mother had been an Air Force nurse stationed there mere weeks before conceiving Athos. They relocated to the United States when Athos was three. His childhood was a jarring string of moves from Air Force town to Air Force town: Mountain Home Air Force Base, Idaho, from age three to seven; Luke Air Force Base in Phoenix, Arizona, which he especially hated, from seven to eleven; Niagara Falls Air Force Base from eleven until he graduated high school.

In Niagara Falls, New York, particularly, he witnessed the disintegration of his parents' marriage along with any barriers that held back his own sadistic tendencies. He did well in school but was friendless. He was teased and bullied frequently – his last name being pronounced *has a pee* leading the reasons – but after a couple of violent retributions, the bullies left him alone. He appreciated the natural beauty of the region – especially the falls themselves – but abhorred the crumbling, corrupt city that festered around it. He found his release in the rural areas north of the city – farm country and the Tuscarora Indian Reservation—in the abundant wildlife there to study, sometimes invasively. The ability to become completely alone if one was willing to bike, or later, drive ten miles north was his oxygen.

Athos' father died when Athos was a junior in high school. Working as a convenience store clerk despite his training, his father found himself on the wrong end of a late-night robbery. His father had been absent from their home for a good three years due to the divorce at the time. Athos never witnessed his mother mourn, but he also never saw her smile again.

Athos deliberately finished third in his class. He despised the idea of giving either a valedictorian or salutatorian speech to his "peers." He would never see any of them again, if he had his way; his time in the Niagara Frontier region was done, and he would never return. Athos started college at SUNY Fredonia but transferred to Cornell University after two years. He graduated with a 4.0 grade average and was accepted to Johns Hopkins in Maryland for Medical School, also completing his residency there after graduation. His time in the "Charm City" focused his direction as a forensic pathologist and budding geneticist. Baltimore both sickened and fascinated him; death and crime were rampant in the city during his time there but a mere sixty-minute drive would place him in rural seclusion again. He frequented Chesapeake Beach as much as possible.

Athos took very few lovers during his time in school and residency; he dabbled in men and women both but found that each lacked anything which appealed to him. He held no particular affection for anyone, and when his mother died a year into his first job – as an entry level lab assistant at the city morgue – he quit and left the United States for Europe without attending her funeral. He retained a lawyer to deal with the inheritance and estate, such as it was.

For decades, Athos bounced around Eastern and Western Europe in equal measure. He avoided Asia altogether due to his prejudice against its peoples. The Baltic States appealed to him the most with their mixture of political upheaval and scenic beauty. The former provided unending opportunity for clandestine, unsanctioned work, and the latter being his only respite.

He was working in Greece when the world came to an end. He had seen it coming very distinctly: one potent coronavirus after another swept up society in waves of pandemic after pandemic. Athos was one of the fortunate few who appeared immune to all strains that had thus far mutated. By the time the economies of both the United States and China had collapsed, there were few people left alive to care. Most parts of the world had already devolved into third-world poverty and anarchy. The collapse of the superpowers opened the door for regional strongmen to assume control of the fiefdoms they'd been eyeing for years.

Athos found favor with a warlord named Casmir who had ended up in charge of Greece – and many of the countries to the north and east of her. Casmir grew up in Slovakia and had no love for naval power, and so he used the Mediterranean, Black, and Adriatic seas as simple borders, then shored up defenses along their coasts. The northern land border of his territory was where he actively kept his armies; his coastal defenses were nearly all automated. His eastern border was secured by a pact of mutually assured destruction with the Turkish warlord Aagha.

Athos had requested a simple base of operations to continue his studies - for the enrichment of Warlord Casmir's purposes, of course – and a small cadre of servants and bodyguards. He was given Parga Castle, and he had grown to love every ancient stone in the place over the intervening years.

Through hundreds of autopsies, necropsies, and more than one violent, live vivisection, Athos had come to understand the fundamentals of how the various coronaviruses continued to not only mutate, but thrive. He was no epidemiologist, however, and so there came a point at which his research had hit a wall. And to the best of his knowledge, every epidemiologist in Europe was dead.

Athos was now ready to overcome that small setback.

A MERE SEVENTY-TWO hours after being dismissed, Mirjet was once again summoned to Athos' laboratory. This time, both Tonys had accompanied him. Each Tony stood just behind each of Mirjet's elbows, ready to subdue or corral him if necessary.

Athos appeared at the other end of the laboratory, seemingly from the walls of the castle itself.

In each of the four hospital beds lay a dark-skinned figure connected to various tubes and IV paraphernalia. Athos could see Mirjet squinting, trying to make sense of what he was seeing across the room.

Patience, Athos thought. *Soon you'll wish you had no eyes with which to see.*

"Ah, Captain Mirjet," Athos called loudly, causing the other man to practically jump backwards. Neither Tony flinched. "I need you to provide Tony there the names of your best four men."

Mirjet briefly moved his eyes back and forth between the two bodyguards flanking him, unsure as to which Tony he should address. The Tony to his right took a small step forward, and Mirjet could see the man held a small notebook. Tony's other hand was poised to write with a small pencil. Mirjet rattled off the names of his two lieutenants, then added the names of his youngest two soldiers.

Tony slipped the notebook into his inside jacket pocket and was out the door before Mirjet had finished speaking the final name.

Athos' voice snapped Mirjet back to attention. "I have one final mission for your group before I release you from my service, Captain. It is very simple, but the details must be followed exactly. You are to descend the castle steps, then head to the beach. There, you will find a small craft to take over water to Ammoudia Beach. It is exactly eight and a half kilometers south-by-southeast. Land on the beach there and journey south for a few meters. There you will find the Acheron River as it flows into the Ionian Sea. In the boat, you will find four ladles. You will take water from the Acheron using these ladles and return directly to this room with them."

Athos noted that Mirjet seemed to relax slightly, this mission description likely less intense than the man had expected.

Athos continued. "You must ensure that you are taking water from the river and not the sea. Move inland if you are worried about which you are obtaining. You must not drink from the water of the Acheron. You must not spill a single drop from a single ladle in transit. You must make it back here with full ladles. If you fail in any aspect of this mission, your remaining men will be killed. Horribly, I might add. And then I will set my sights on tracking you and your remaining four men down. I cannot stress enough how important it is that you neither spill, nor drink, Acheron's water."

Athos arched his eyebrow as if waiting.

Mirjet was no longer relaxed.

"Do you understand these orders, Captain?" Athos recognized that Mirjet voiced no objection to the incorrect ranking; the man had never been higher than a Sergeant in the *SHISH*. He could have been the King of Albania for all it mattered.

"Yes, yes sir, I do. I will impress this upon my men."

"Good." There was a single knock upon the door. "Ah, there's Tony with your *four best men*." Athos' tone straddled mocking and earnestness. "Please make haste, Captain. *Carefully*."

Mirjet nearly stumbled over the Tony to his left in his effort to flee the laboratory.

After the captain was gone, the remaining Tony inclined his head slightly toward Athos.

"Go. Make watch for their return." Athos ordered.

One sharp nod and Tony was out the door, and Athos was once again alone.

ATHOS SPENT the next two hours busying himself with the figures in the hospital beds. Each was still, but there were monitors of all types surrounding each one, lights blinking red and green. The EKG in each berth was silent but showed a chilling straight blue line for each body.

Tony leaned into the lab and waited until Athos looked up from his duties. "Sir, they have landed on our beach. They will be making their way up the castle steps soon."

"Thank you, Tony." Athos nodded. "Please show Mirjet and his team directly here and then guard them, please."

Tony nodded, not betraying the fact that he had no idea what Athos had planned for the five men, and leaned out of the lab again.

Athos resumed checking each berth, this time fussing with the IV poles; each had multiple ports with syringes poised to deliver whatever medication was held within.

Satisfied, Athos took a seat to the left of the berths. He was slightly in the shadows, as each berth was lit from above by industrial grade lights. He heard a light commotion outside of the lab's door. Tony stuck his head back in and, apparently satisfied that Athos was a good enough distance away, allowed the men into the laboratory.

Mirjet walked in first, his gait slow. His attention was on the men slowly filing in behind him. Each successive *SHISH* soldier had their eyes fixed on the metal ladle in their hands, their treads soft and their faces reverent, blocking all else out. Athos could have been on fire and they wouldn't have noticed. "Sir, as ordered," Mirjet said gently.

Athos shot to his feet and boomed out a jovial "Excellent!" Some of the men looked up, but immediately returned their widened eyes to the ladles. The Tonys took up position blocking the exit door, each with a suppressed 9mm pistol behind their backs. To the other men, they simply seemed to be standing at attention. That is, if the other men even noticed them.

Athos gestured to the man at the right end of the formation. "Come here, soldier." Athos picked up a roughly made earthenware cup from a nearby table. "Pour that precious water into this cup."

The Albanian did as told, then turned this way and that, confused as to what to do with his now-empty ladle. It was clear he wanted it out of his possession as quickly as possible.

Athos, turned his back to the man. "On the table," he said dismissively. He approached the first berth, holding the cup in both of his hands. He was aware of the other men in the room, but his attention was now fully focused on the body in the berth's bed. One of the Tonys had questioned Mirjet extensively about the contents of each box his men had borne up the castle's steps. This bed held a middle-aged male from the WHO compound. According to the small 3x5 card that Athos had placed on the bed next the body's covered legs, this man had been employed in the Information Technology area of the WHO.

Athos looked down at the man with an almost loving look. The man's skin was a mixture of gray and green; he had been found on his back, so all of the blood had pooled there. If Athos were to flip the man over, he would see nothing but onyx skin. It was difficult to tell anything about the man not provided on the 3x5 card. His face was as bloated as the rest of his body. His tongue conveniently bulged out past his swollen lips, giving Athos an eternal raspberry.

It was finally time.

Athos gently parted the man's upper lip from his tongue and poured some of the water from River Acheron into his dead mouth, then waited a moment before taking a cautionary step back.

Commotion filled the lab at once. The dead man sputtered, a good amount of the water flying into the air and coming back down to splash his tumid face. His eyes opened wide and stayed that way without blinking. A gurgling roar started, seemingly centered in his chest.

Most of Mirjet's company, including Mirjet, issued shocked cries. One of the men pitched forward in an attempt to catch his fumbled ladle, but only succeeded in causing the water to spill. The ladle hit the floor with a resounding clatter. The leftmost Tony stepped forward, leveled his suppressed pistol at the man's temple and fired a round into his head. The soldier's blood and brain matter bathed Mirjet's face as he bent at the knee to help steady the man. Mirjet slowly stood and, when it became apparent that he was not the next to die, stepped back into line and stood as stiffly as possible, eyes forward.

Tony stepped back into position to the left of the other Tony as if nothing had happened.

Athos crossed at the foot of the bed to the other side and immediately pressed the plunger on a syringe full of brownish liquid which traveled through the IV tubes into the man's body. By now, the man was lightly convulsing from side to side, his eyes straining. He appeared to be trying to look around him, but his muscles were still frozen, and so all he could do was stiffly flop from side to side. The gurgling roar had turned to a full-throated scream by now, inarticulate and filled with agony.

Something appeared to change in the man's stiffness, as his upper body was now thrashing to the right while his legs were doing the opposite. A sound like a large, dry cloth being ripped was audible under the unnerving screams. A massive brown-red stain appeared on the white sheets over his midsection and spread rapidly.

Finally, the man arched his back in a way that seemed physically impossible to those watching the spectacle. His stomach and pelvis were thrust into the air while his feet and head drilled down into the soft white of the hospital bed. Then his desperate scream died in his dead throat and tapered to a deep burble as his body crashed to a prone position. Some viscera projected from both his mouth and his torn torso, and then he was still.

Athos stood with his head bowed and a single index finger covering his lips. He appeared to be either deep in thought or simply willing the dead man to remain quiet. The men in the room were still. The smell of urine wafted from the pant leg of one of the soldiers.

Athos then turned toward the men and pursed his lips. He started to speak, paused to notice the dead soldier missing a quarter of his skull, and then continued.

"What you have just witnessed is me bringing a man back from the dead. I accomplished this with a concoction of my own making. The last ingredient is from the Acheron River, as you can see. If you recall your school lessons, the Acheron is the river that joined with several other rivers in the Underworld to form the river Styx. I administered a fatal overdose of heroin to deliver him once again to death's embrace. He was, after all, simply a test case and not someone who could provide me with the information I need.

"These three other bodies you brought from Geneva, however, *do* possess information that I greatly desire. Together, they are among the foremost epidemiologists, virologists and infectious disease doctors from the *double-you aitch oh*. Or, at least the ones that had died the most recently.

"Your colleague--" Athos directed his gaze to the dead soldier briefly— "did not demonstrate the same, well, *mettle* that the rest of you have. That is why you are still alive. You will remain here while I revive and question the last three corpses. Once my research is complete – it should only be a day or two – I will then inoculate the five, er, the *four* of you against the coming waves of disease as this coronavirus continues to mutate. I will charge you with bringing a sample of this vaccine to the warlord Aagha, who rules Turkey and beyond, as a gesture of goodwill. You shall be harbingers of my success, starting with Istanbul!"

Relief seemed to settle over the collected soldiery, although Mirjet's gaze remained stern and focused on the middle distance, blood still dripping from his face and hair. The first soldier briefly looked heavenward and exhaled deeply. The other two refreshed the grips of their ladles and settled in for more screams.

A WEEK LATER, Athos watched the three soldiers and Mirjet – all freshly injected with what Athos had developed in his lab - make their way down the steps of Castle Parga. Each of the Tonys flanked him. Athos gestured for them both to come forward and face him. Next to him, on his right, a small table held a sweating glass of iced tea.

"I want to commend you both on your excellent work this past few months."

"Thank you, sir," they said in unison.

"Do either of you have any questions about what we've accomplished, now that this mission is complete?"

Both Tonys remained stoic, but after a few moments of thought, one of the Tonys – the one to Athos' right – allowed his lip to twitch.

"Please, Tony, you are my trusted bodyguard. I don't want there to be any confusion here. Speak, I insist."

"Sir. Yes, sir, forgive me for this question."

Athos waved his left hand and favored the rightmost Tony with a small smile.

"Sir, why would you allow those men who have both intimate knowledge of this stronghold and...more importantly, this vaccine, to go to your master's enemy? Is Casmir really extending an olive branch to the Turks?"

"Ah, there it is." Athos nodded amiably. "The question I was looking for. Well, Tony, here's what those men actually took with them: I engineered an even deadlier virus than the one we're currently facing. Those men have been injected with it but won't likely become symptomatic for three to five days. I'm counting on them finding audience with Aagha, or at least his close lieutenants, and infecting them before then. This should bring down Aagha's entire fiefdom, either way."

The rightmost Tony was at a loss for words, and his face turned utterly white.

Athos flicked his eyes to the leftmost Tony, who immediately took a single step backward, unholstered his pistol, and blew the head off the other Tony.

Athos had covered the top of the iced tea with his palm to avoid it being sullied. He gently picked it up and took a sip. "Thank you, Tony."

Acknowledgments

The author would like to thank the following people, in no particular order:

My incredibly talented wife, the author Aly Welch, my other incredibly talented wife, the artist and writer Tom Rolland, Josh Marshall, Jeff Naab, Cari + Ed Dubiel, Kaytalin + Scott McCarry, Patrick Delaney, G.A. Finocchiaro, Evan Graham, John Christian, Peter L. Harmon, Susan K. Hamilton, S.E. Soldwedel, Jason Pomerance, T.C.C. Edwards, R.H. Webster, Tahani Nelson, Darla Bubar, Dan & Jenn Sinclair, Radoslav Kostura, Gavin Loudon, Christer Samslått, Will (Ripped), Carolyn Markowski & Daniel Keleher, Holly @ Lock City Books in Lockport, NY

To all of the amazing people that have been kind enough to read & post reviews about my work – thank you! Without you, I'm a pebble tossed into the Pacific without as much as a tiny *sploosh*. My eternal gratitude extends to the following people, with their Instagram tags in parentheses: Nicole (twice_booked), Kiera (thathorrorbish), Brandy (horrorbookwhore), Melissa (books_booze_horror), Andi (spooky_booknerd_4ever), Ashley Nestler, MSW (the_horror_maven), Eileen Bailey (eileen.reads.horror), Casey (bookish.horror.gemini), Ashley Ingram (spookylittlebooknerd), Rebbie (rebbiereviews), Shelby (abookishpage), Samantha Hargrove (expertbooksmuggler), C.J. Daley (cjdscurrentread), Gwendolyn (gwenreadshorror), Rose (rosedevoursbooks), Mariah (the.bookish.ghoul), Michelle Jones (horrorbook.hellhound), (TheseHauntedPages), Amy (ravensreadingbooks), Brittany (horror_haus_books), Heather Miller (hmillerhorror), S.C. (dreadfully.grim), Maddy (maddy.reads.books), Karla Kay (karlas.literary.korner), Rebecca

Rossi (my_bookish_universe), Ric (life_in_books_ric), Jon (reading_with_jon), Pan (undead_dad_reads), Drea Scott (dreasbones_reads), (horrorbookstagram), and last but never least, Tony Jones of Ginger Nuts of Horror (gnofhorror.com)

I am eternally inspired by the writing of: John Skipp, Craig Spector, Stephen King, Anne Rice (rest in peace, Queen), Cormac McCarthy (rest in peace, King), Irvine Welsh, Glen Duncan & Brian K. Vaughan

I am constantly listening to the music of: Thom Yorke & Radiohead, Wolf Alice, Assemblage23, Interpol, Run the Jewels, Metric, The Cure, The Smiths, and lately, Wet Leg.

About the Author

Mike X Welch resides in his native Western New York with his wife, the author Aly Welch and their twin teenage sons. His adult daughter resides near Seattle with her iconoclast ways and does the cosplays well enough to make your head swim. When not writing, staring at his computer in abject depression, or cheerleading his wife's ability to knock out a novel per year, Welch fixes computers for a living. He enjoys his five cats, his many rats, and his new puppy, Glory. He worries that he and Aly are now officially out of pet names taken from the Buffy & Angel TV series, and other first world problems. He masochistically supports the Buffalo Bills & the Buffalo Sabres.

Welch is now at work on his next project: *A History of Blood*. This will be a millennia-spanning horror novel featuring a vampire, a djinn, and the goddess Kali. He also continues to work with the incredible folks at Duskbound Books in his capacity as Author Wrangler and Anthology Coordinator, both job titles that actually mean "cat herder." You can visit www.mikexwelch.com, but his lazy ass probably hasn't updated it since 2021. Instead, go to DuskboundBooks.com

ABOUT THE ARTIST

Tom Rolland is an illustrator and novelist from Glasgow, Scotland. He has a passion for streetscape and life-drawing, but his guilty pleasure is comic art. He lives with his beautiful wife and daughters and wants for nothing. Rolland's favorite author is a fella called Mike X Welch and his loftiest creative aspiration is to draw pictures of the aforementioned writer's quirky, creepy tales of the unexpected and macabre.

DUSKBOUND
BOOKS

Duskbound Books is run by a team of book-loving professionals. Founded by Kaytalin McCarry, Cari Dubiel, G.A. Finocchiaro, Aly Welch and Mike X Welch, Duskbound is a unique hybrid publisher with a vision for helping independent authors achieve their publishing dreams.

Duskbound Books has two strategic arms:
Publishing
and
Publication Services
For more information on these, please visit:
https://duskboundbooks.com/services/

Lastly, this is a book produced by an independent publisher. We live and die by reviews on sites such as Amazon, Goodreads, and more. We ask that you please take the time to leave an honest review on one of the aforementioned sites. It really can make all the difference in the world. Thank you, and happy reading!

Find us at:
DuskboundBooks.com
Instagram: @duskboundbooks
Facebook: /duskboundbooks

The original, abbreviated version of "Turning of the Bones" appeared in *ENANTIODROMIA: Collected Stories* (Amazon 2020)

"You Might Get It" appeared in Writing Bloc's *Deception* anthology (2019) and also in *ENANTIODROMIA*

"Tuesdays with Moran'd'arth" originally appeared in *ENANTIODROMIA*

"Bizarre Love Triangle" originally appeared in the Writing Bloc anthology *PASSAGEWAYS: Mythos* (2023)

"The Necromancer of Parga" originally appeared in the High Dive Publishing anthology *Horror from the High Dive, Vol. 2* (2022)

This book is to be played loud or not at all

Printed in Great Britain
by Amazon

45137630R00088